The
BASTARDIZER

THE BASTARDIZER'S CHRONICLES

THE BASTARDIZER POLISHES A TURD

by
"CHUS MARTINEZ"

pictures by Sönke Rickertsen

CRIPPLEGATE BOOKS, LONDON   2022

Written entirely on location in Collingwood,

Victoria, Australia, on Country of the

Wurundjeri and Boonwurrung people.

Sovereignty was never ceded.

Published by

Cripplegate Books

London

Set in Perpetua, Gill Sans and
Grotesque No. 9 No. 9 No. 9.

BOOK PRODUCTION
WAR ECONOMY STANDARD

This book is produced in complete
conformity with the authorized
economy standards

This book is dedicated to

the life and works

of

FLANN O'BRIEN

&

WILHELM REICH

CHUS MARTINEZ SAYS

Big Shout Out to **Stewart Home** and all the visionaries at Cripplegate Books who bought this manuscript sight unseen when I accidentally unearthed it long ago on 2nd September 2021. Thanks for all your patience whilst we got the revisions and citations and illustrations sorted.

Blessings of the Highest Order to the talented polymath **Sönke Rickertsen** for the groovy illustrations and the accompanying soundtrack. Cheers for your casual disregard of any kind of adherence to the brief at hand. You captured the mood perfectly.

Ta very much to **Alex Gionfriddo** too, whose fantastic drawings sadly hit the cutting room floor but will look fab in the inevitable deluxe expanded edition.

Grudging thanks to the indefatigable **Sir Simon Strong** for the overly comprehensive index and the lovely unhelpful diagrams.

I couldn't have done it without your support and encouragement. So you're all implicated when the shit hits the fan. Cheers anyway. This is **Chus Martinez**. We play rock and roll,

1.2.3.4.

On the spur of a mad moment one does crazy things which, reviewed in the light of experience often seem to open the floodgates of self-destruction. The valiant soul tries to compensate by performing super-human feats to counteract foolishness. The run-of-the-mill types get uptight and fall apart. I have always considered myself resilient. Under the circumstances it is just as well that some mysterious power of self-preservation burns bright within my writing "heart".

When L_____ B_____ of Cripplegate Books threw the idea of becoming his fiction editor at me I instantly accepted the invitation. In the cold light of after-the-fact reasoning this was really asking for trouble. L_____ knew several of my close friends who nursed writing ambitions and it did not surprise me when I found their efforts in the pile of manuscripts that had been dumped on my desk. It didn't take long to sort through the submissions. First of all I threw out everything that was over sixty thousand words in length. Next, I went through the covering letters that accompanied the manuscripts. Seven would-be authors were rejected for making references to their "art", twenty-four for mentioning writers I don't like and one for using the word "caveat". I was able to eliminate another two authors because of their posh double-barrelled surnames and a third for being called Rupert. After twenty minutes work I was left with just one possible candidate for publication: *The Bastardizer Polishes a Turd* by Chus Martinez.

My heart sunk, I'd never yet read a decent line of fiction by an unpublished author who was also a personal acquaintance. Cripplegate had to publish something and Chus's manuscript was the only thing to survive my rigorous selection process. I settled down to read the text and in the first tense ticking-off seconds I knew my reputation hung in the balance. Fortunately, *The Bastardizer Polishes a Turd* was the best novel I'd read by a British author in years! What I am doing in seeing this book through to publication is not nepotism. For too long the paperback author has resided in a wilderness remote from "literary" acclaim. The writers who "slave" to bring the reading public entertainment at a reasonable price are the backbone of an industry geared to honour those for whom the "bell should not always toll". Far too many critics devote lengthy passages to books ghosted for this, or that, personality. "Ghosted" by the real pro, I may add. Others are subjected to adulation when, in fact, their efforts are the result of editorial revision which turns a moderate manuscript into a work of genius.

Chus Martinez isn't going to win the Nobel Prize for Literature, I wouldn't want to be involved with anything likely to win "accolades" of that type!

Instead, *The Bastardizer Polishes a Turd* gives fiction back the bad name it needs in these days of literary respectability and the hype surrounding the inflated advances given to authors who have singularly failed to sink their teeth into the task of re-inventing world culture in its entirety. What does the reading public really want, the effete twitterings of the Oxbridge "elite" or the no-holds-barred pulp-splatter of Chus Martinez? History will vindicate my judgement…

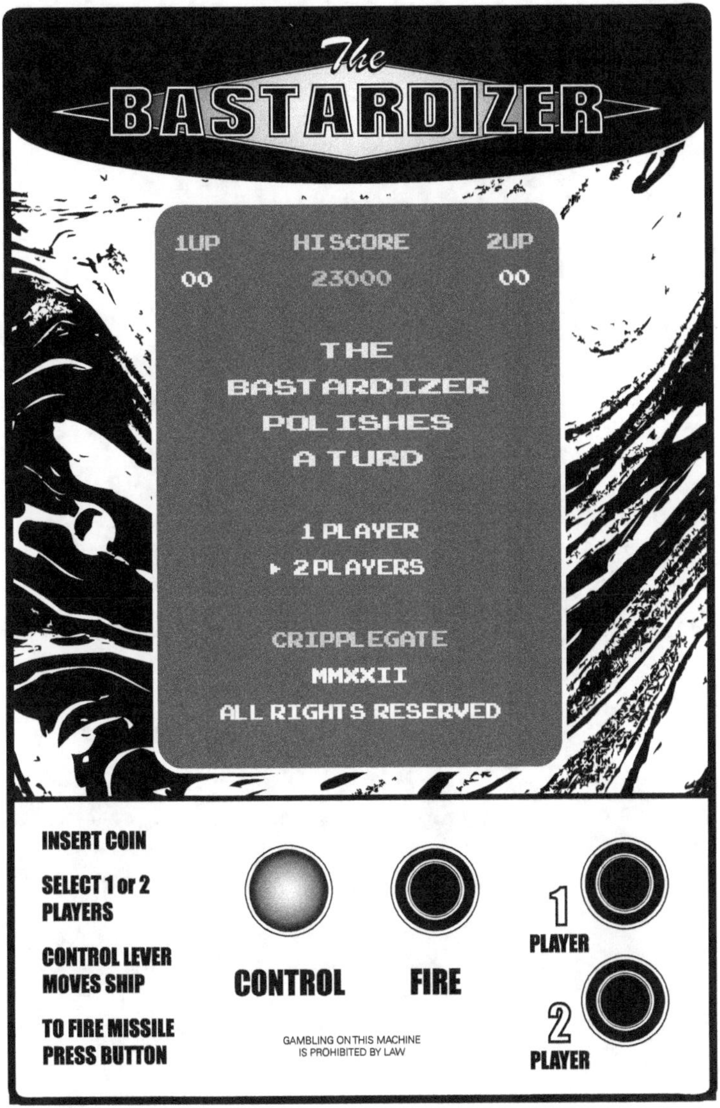

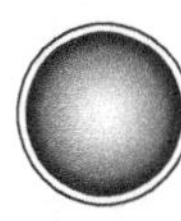

The BASTARDIZER
1UP   HI SCORE   2UP
00   23000   00
THE
BASTARDIZER
POLISHES
A TURD
1 PLAYER
▸ 2 PLAYERS
CRIPPLEGATE
MMXXII
ALL RIGHTS RESERVED
INSERT COIN
SELECT 1 or 2 PLAYERS
CONTROL LEVER MOVES SHIP
TO FIRE MISSILE PRESS BUTTON
CONTROL
FIRE
1 PLAYER
2 PLAYER
GAMBLING ON THIS MACHINE
IS PROHIBITED BY LAW

"SO WHY HAVE YOU WRITTEN ALL THIS?" YOU ASK ME... "YOU CRAVE LIFE YET ATTEMPT TO UNRAVEL ITS MEANINGS WITH MUDDLED LOGIC. HOW TROUBLESOME, HOW RUDE ARE YOUR OUTBURSTS, AND YET AT THE SAME TIME HOW FRIGHTENED YOU ARE! YOU TALK NONSENSE AND ARE DELIGHTED WITH IT; YOU MAKE OUTRAGEOUS REMARKS YET ARE ALARMED BY THEM AND ARE FOREVER APOLOGISING. YOU PROFESS TO FEAR NOTHING AND AT THE SAME TIME COME CRINGING TO US FOR OUR APPROVAL. YOU PROFESS TO BE GNASHING YOUR TEETH WHILE AT THE SAME TIME YOU CRACK JOKES TO ENTERTAIN US. YOU KNOW THAT YOUR JOKES ARE NOT FUNNY, YET YOU ARE CLEARLY PLEASED WITH YOU CLEVERNESS. THERE MAY BE TRUTH IN YOU, BUT YOU HAVE NO MODESTY; OUT OF THE PETTIEST VANITY YOU DISPLAY AND DEGRADE YOUR INTEGRITY IN THE MARKETPLACE... YOU REALLY DO WANT TO SAY SOMETHING BUT CONTINUE TO PREVARICATE BECAUSE YOU HAVE NO COURAGE, ONLY COWARDLY IMPUDENCE. YOU SOUND OFF ABOUT YOUR AWARENESS YET CONTINUE TO WAVER, BECAUSE ALTHOUGH YOUR BRAIN IS WORKING YOUR HEART IS DARK WITH CORRUPTION. AND WITHOUT A PURE HEART THERE CAN BE NO REAL AWARENESS. AND HOW PERSISTENT, HOW PERSEVERING, HOW PRETENTIOUS YOU ARE. LIES, LIES, LIES!" OF COURSE I MYSELF HAVE MADE UP THESE WORDS OF YOURS. *F.D.*

FUCK THE LOT OF YOU!!!

An Old Age Pornographer awoke with a start—as if there was any other way to. The ceiling was revolving. The floor was rotating. The walls were spinning. It was business as usual then. A Vickers Viscount was taking off somewhere. He lay there in his rancid pit lovely and comfy and snug and he hoped that none of it was real.

Then, with a superhuman effort that he deserved a medal for, the old cunt prised open his rheumy crybones and the first thing he saw as usual was that book (A) that was still there on the bedside table. It had a cover, half-title, title page, reverse-title page with all the imprimatur and finally the opening paragraph… overdue but as inevitable as a big fucking bastard.

Sadly the book in question was in a language that the wizened exotic novelist couldn't read anyway, but that just made it a better cure for his crushing insomnia. Other useless shit also cluttered the wonky pedestal too: (B) a goose-neck aluminium lamp made by an Italian P OWs in 1943, its bulb had burned out years before and you couldn't get them anymore but since his electric had been cut off none of that mattered; (C) a can of insecticide, effective not just on flies but more importantly on mosquitoes and hornets and swarms of other things named after WWII aeroplanes, or at least it would have been if it wasn't empty which it was. Some of the insects it was effective against were

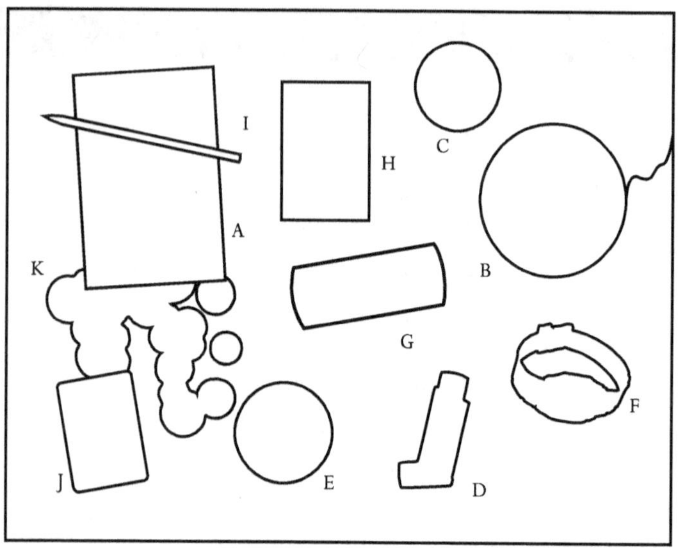

extinct by now anyway; (D) an asthma puffer which he only needed if he used the fly-spray, and that was empty too but it had a little propellant left in so at least it made a reassuring noise; (E) a cracked tumbler that smelled of stale lager, not enough residue to get a mosquito pissed even; (F) a Taiwanese digital watch from a petrol station. Seven of the 42 segments of the LED display had burned out so the length of time you needed to look at it to read the time varied depending on the configuration; (G) the cardboard core from a toilet roll not that he issued tears or jism on a regular schedule anymore. There was a notebook (H) too, its pages were filled with scribbles done pissed in the middle of the night and not even the author could discern them afterwards. It didn't matter, since often he'd awake and scribble over the pages he'd already filled up without seeing so the layers of gibberish built up and up but now no longer now since his pen (I) had inevitably run out. (J) A deck of cards with one missing. Guess which? And (K) a pile of foreign coins from countries he'd never been to and some of which didn't even exist anymore. They were weird sizes and colours. These were the leftovers that he'd never been able to pass off in local shops or vending machines.

The combination of items on the table had taken years to develop. It seemed sad that none of the items could fulfil their intended task now but at times in the past some of the items hadn't even been there to be useless. Nevertheless, sometimes the sozzled old hack felt sorry for himself.

25:07:1956

Located somewhere between Korea and the Bay of Pigs, the not very United States of the middle-third of north America farted explosively and almost loud enough to rouse itself from its own sticky dreams for once.

The sheets were damp and the radio had switched on by itself. It was the middle of the night and what they used to call Race Music started blasting out through the gingham and glass of the kitchen windows and out across the sumbering sluburbs. Folks across the epidermal spectrum woke up suddenly and started fucking in droves and the following morning no other music was tolerated. And it wasn't like the recycled

diluted rock-n-roll we have now—this was akin to white lightning from bootleg stills that could send you blind if you drank
it wrong. In the coming years the feedback loop from the first
wave of rock-n-rollers to the imminent British Invasion would
be sold back to gullible Yanks like an antibiotic to sanitise the
form but first another experimental recuperative technique
would have to be tried.

Deejays Dickie Goodman and Bill Buchanan were invoked
and spontaneously recorded "The Flying Saucer" the first
widely-heard example of sampling in popular music. Digital
audio technologies didn't exist at the time and they
manifested their then-topical alien invasion
skit with rudimentary equipment from fragments of popular records; for which they
were abruptly sued for multiple copyright
infringements. Their record label came to
an agreement with the publishers of the
original songs and the record went on to
sell close to a million copies spawning a whole
genre of "break-in" or "snippet" records. The hit
record also served to boost sales of the sampled songs and
spurred interest in their creators, many of whom were Af-
rican-American singers whose original renditions had never
been heard by a mainstream (then a euphemism for "white"-
skinned) audience.

Meanwhile, the catastrophic side-effects of this prototypi-
cal culture-jam would take another three decades to con-
cretely manifest themselves.

The life of a copyright enforcement agent might hypothetically be described as months of terror punctuated by moments of extreme boredom. I went in a café, sat down and the girl came over to take my order.

"Bring me a bacon sandwich and step on it!" I went.

There was a tape playing. It was "Male Stripper" by Man2Man Meets Man Parrish. The song cut out midway through.

"I want to see the manager," I went, furthermore.

"He's out the back," she went.

"Get him," I went.

She went and got him. He was a big cunt in a shell-suit.

"Yeah, what?" He went, eloquently.

"What's that tape what's playing?" I asked him.

"What tape?" He went.

The girl got the tape out of the machine. "What? This?" She went, waving it at me naively.

"Yeah" I went. "That." It was a TDK C90AD. The tune had obviously been taped off the radio.

"I don't fucking know," she went huffily, "some guy left it here…"

"Some guy!" I went… "Some Guy!? Home Taping is Killing Music!!!" I pulled out my piece and shoved it into the manager-cunt's cake-hole taking out a couple of teeth on the way through.

I PULLED OUT MY PIECE AND SHOVED IT INTO THE
MANAGER-CUNT'S CAKE-HOLE TAKING OUT A COUPLE
OF TEETH ON THE WAY THROUGH.

"But as far as I'm concerned Home Taping is KILL-ING MUSIC!! Haven't you even fucking heard of the Copyright Act 1956 proscribing the reproduction of copyright works without their owner's specific permission? In writing!" I threw the cunt over the counter and waved my piece around a bit.

The only other customer in the joint was an old dosser in the corner and he chose this moment to make his exit. Without paying! The cheap cunt. But I had no time for that kind of nonsense. It was outside my brief. In this game you gotta know how to focus.

"And I don't see any license displayed prominently neither. I take it you do have a license for the public performance of recorded works?" I was foaming at the mouth and bits of spit and crap flew out of my gob. In fact it was a good job I'd not actually had the bacon sarnie since that would have been gross. The fat cunt himself proceeded to dribble blood and the occasional bit of broken tooth.

"Yuh… nuh… guh…" he gibbered.

"Fuck it." I went and gave him a swift but effective boot to the bollocks. Hard. He was so fucked up he didn't even feel it. So I did it again. He kinda registered it that time. By then I was famished so I went to get a burger down the road.

The 22nd of November 1963 was a relatively eventful day. In the UK, for example, The Beatles issued their second album *With The Beatles* to a hysterical popular and critical reaction. Whilst on the other side of the Atlantic Stanley Kubrick's *Dr Strangelove* was getting its first test screening and the 35th President of the USA was being shot in the head and reputedly killed. Concerned that this latter event would distract viewers the BBC postponed broadcast of their revolutionary

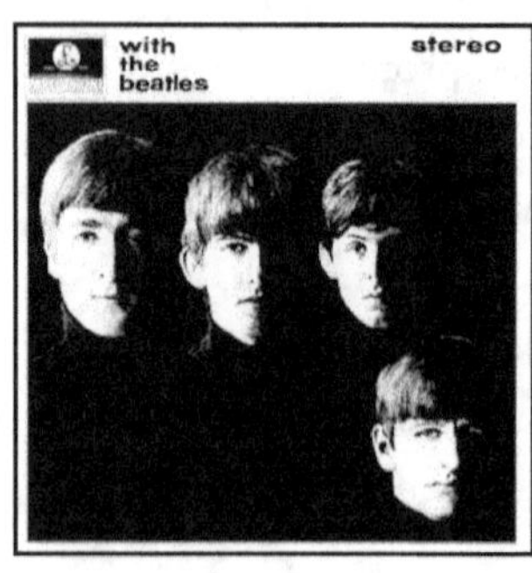

new SF show called *Dr Who* until the next day. Three of these four events are often inextricably associated in the minds of those old enough to recall them and others who just know about them anyway.

Over the next 23 years a bunch of mostly terrible JFK-related tunes would be realised. The first of these, The Byrds' "He Was a Friend of Mine" was supposedly written the day of the shooting and was a reworking of a folk standard dating back to at least December 1933 when John Lomax recorded James "Iron Head" Baker singing "Shorty George" at Central State Prison Farm in Sugar Land, Texas. McGuinn's lyrics—"From a sixth floor window a gunman shot him down"—indicated that the singer concurred with the findings of the Warren Commission that JFK had been killed by Lee Harvey Oswald acting alone.

This opinion was squarely contradicted by David Crosby when the group played the Monterey Pop Festival in California on Saturday 17 June 1967. In an inter-tune interjection prior to their JFK tribute he alleged:

> I'm sure that they'll edit this out. When President Kennedy was killed, he was not killed by one man. He was shot from a number of different directions by different guns. The story has been suppressed, witnesses have been killed, and this is your country, ladies and gentlemen.

Crosby explicably left the group shortly afterwards.

Probably the most cynical monstrosity, and the first JFK mash-up, arrived in 1971 when Tom Clay, purported associate of Marilyn Monroe and discredited founder of the spurious Beatles Booster Clubs, assembled "What the World Needs Now/Abraham, Martin and John" from covers of the two songs by session musos combined with radio soundbites from the Kennedy assassinations and Martin Luther King's mountain-top speech. This sonic abomination went to number eight in the US charts so someone must have liked it.

Understandably, most of the tributes to JFK were from US-based artists but it's interesting to recall the cluster of British artists jumping on the motorcade bandwagon a decade-and-a-half later. It became customary not to make promo clips for these tributes though, so the Zapruder footage became a de-facto promo-video for all of em.

Redemption for the meme remained unpostulated until 23 years later when NYC DJ Steinski created his radical sonic montage of the fateful day's news broadcasts: "The Motorcade Sped On". Tommy Boy Records were unable to obtain clearances for the use of Walter Cronkite's voice and abandoned any official release. The recording surfaced in a samizdat white label edition and copies were bizarrely given away free with the *New Musical Express* in February 1987. The tune would become the modern prototype of a strange and exciting new genre.

UNHAD SARNIE FALLOUT

The following day I was sitting in my office with my secretary. Suddenly, a klaxon sounded outside in the street. I jumped to my feet and screamed "What's a klaxon?"

It turned out that the noise was the gaffer calling me into his office. When I got there you could cut the atmosphere with a specially designed atmosphere cutting machine that would probably be manufactured in Germany. The chief seemed disgruntled about something.

"There have been a number of… uh… reports recently about your conduct. Uh… strange, or maybe odd, things. Unsubstantiated of course."

"I call it as I see it, Chief," I went.

"Well, quite. Yes. But nevertheless…"

I figured I should put my cards on the table. "And this is the way I see it, Chief. We're out there to do a job. It's a—I was going to say dirty but I won't—job. And if I don't do it someone else will! Listen. Here is a man who could not take any more. If not now when? If not you, who? Tomorrow, someone else. But this job is hard! And it takes a hard man to do it! And a hard man is hard to find! And if that makes me a monster then I'm a monster!!! If you want my badge and my gun, you can have them. I don't need them anymore."

"Well, I was going to come to that. You see, one of the strange things is that we don't actually have badges in the Copyright and Intellectual Property Enforcement Squad. We have these uh laminated cards instead," he tossed his ID over the desk at me. "And for a second thing: we don't generally go armed."

"You don't mean to suggest that I go up against these… scum… armed with nothing but a piece of plasticised cardboard? It's not even cardboard more like cartridge paper!" I waved the card in his ugly mug and he snatched it back off me rudely.

"That's precisely what I'd suggest. You do have one? Don't you?"

"Errr… well, now that you mention it, Chief."

"I see…" The Chief hmmmmed, "Well, that would explain a number of things… You don't actually work for this Department do you?"

"I work harder than anyone for this Department!"

"No, you miss my point. I meant to imply that I suspected that you weren't officially in the employ of this Department."

"Well, Chief, I'm awfully sorry, but I'm just not very good at 'official'. Like the copyright violating filth I see out there on the streets every day. How 'official' is their despicable thievery?"

"Well then, let me put it to you like this," he went. "Why don't you just get out of my office and out of this Department and out of my life forever," he elaborated. "You cunt. And if I ever catch you on my manor again your arse will be toast so fast your feet won't reach the floor."

I don't usually eat toast with my arse but I got the picture and I was going anyway. I still had my badge and my gun. Result.

I went out of the HQ into the street and took a butchers around the old shithole. I suddenly wondered how strip-tease artists were protecting their sexy routines from illegal exploitation and thought I should find a strip-joint to investigate. By the time I got there it was academic since The Stripper had just finished her routine. A home-made air-hostess uniform lay discarded and the grotty stage was slick with baby oil and littered with sweet wrappers. I could only speculate as to what her act had involved and could only hope that it didn't involve any cocoa-based trademark infringement. The professional ecdysiast was wandering round the boozer with all her bits out and a pint tankard filled with mostly silver but intermittently gold coins. She must have been good.

WAITING FOR THE GLUEMAN

Now the old wankthropologist was lying on his back on the kitchen floor thinking about the many happy hours he had spent lying on his back on the kitchen floor. He spent most of his waking hours experimenting with home-made bongs and watching as much telly as his retinas could stand, the shitter the better, and sometimes tenth-gen seventies pornos when he could be arsed going in the other room to get the tapes. This meagre fare was occasionally supplanted with half-kilo bags of generic tortilla chips and a six-pack of extra-strength lager, preferably dumped cheap from some Eastern Bloc country. Furthermore, he hadn't had a woman in a decade or a fight in half that or a drink since last night despite that.

So thus the lines were drawn and the old bastard lumbered up from where he'd last collapsed like he was Godzilla or something. He squinted and tried to get his bloodshot eyes to focus on something as he bounced limply off the walls heading for the khazi to piss. He couldn't even be bothered putting a micturition joke in here. Whilst there he took the opportunity to retch and hack up a great yellow loogie of something which he spat in what he hoped was the direction of the toilet bowl. I expect he missed. Then he went back and skinned up a couple for the road, necked something from the dregs of a glass and pocketed the leftover stubby to drink the balance on the way as he stumbled downstairs and fumbled with the lock. The winter blasted him as he exited into the night. Stars and streetlamps were indistinguishable to his knackered eyesight. A pig chopper went over with a searchlight beaming through the pea-souper inna 1942 blitz stylee catching the towers of the city on the horizon. It didn't matter which one.

"Fuckin barrage balloons," he went spontaneously.

As he ambled, he thought he was whistling the opening bars of "For What it's Worth" by Buffalo Springfield but actually he was just wheezing asthmatically in time with what he thought was the tune since he'd lost the ability to whistle a few years previously.

Meanwhile, a trinity of hard lads from the primary school were chroming under the footbridge as he turned into the main road. One of them had managed to glue his head inside a carrier bag and his pals were pointing at him and laughing. When they saw the old fucker coming one of them yelled "What a shocking bad hat!" and lobbed an empty aerosol at him.

The old writer weighed up the odds and before he knew it his wizened fist connected with the face of the first child—who would have been safe if he'd been in school like he should have been. There's a lesson there. The poor kid's nose has been weakened by years of glue-love and now it collapsed like a wank-basted tissue. Sorry about that. Then the second came at him brandishing a flick-knife.

"Call that brandishing?!" went the re-invigorated old fuck, "I'll fucking brandish you," and the chiselled toe-tip of his winklepicker—sole flapping like the tongue of a rabid dachshund—found its mark satisfyingly square in the centre of the knackers of the dork.

"Gnnnnnggg!" went the thuglet, thrifty with vowels and simultaneously using the minimum configuration of consonants too. It would be some time before that epithet would be admissible in Scrabble! The third "tough" stayed were he was, observant, and then he micturated himself into blessed unconsciousness, rendered insensible by the spectacle of his comrades' misfortunes and neutered by the invocation of those scare quotes.

FUCKING SHITHOUSE APOLOGY FOR A SHOE!

"Not a bad start!" Reckoned the gratuitously violent old fuck as he sauntered on; more jauntily now.

THE BANALITY OF EVIL

It was then that my piece chose to accidentally discharge. The shot went straight into the cassette player over the bar. Fragments of plastic shrapnel shot all over the place and the tape spooled itself out onto the floor like the deck was spewing out lungfuls of blood or entrails or something. Obviously the tune came to an abrupt end at this point. An astonished looking white guy with dreadlocks looked at me astonished.

"…the fuck?" He went.

I improvised and went into my customary damage-limitation routine. "(I) That cassette constitutes unlawful reproduction of a copyright work. (ii) You are committing a criminal offence by publicly disseminating a copyright work without permission and without payment of royalties and associated fees. (iii) This venue is not licensed by the relevant authority for public performances (iv) or dancing, if that's what it was (v) or music for that matter, and (vi) say your prayers, motherfucker!" And I punched the cunt in the gut and he doubled so I kneed him in the teeth while he was there and he keeled over backwards. I grabbed his greasy dreads and spun him round on the beery ground so he was kneeling in front of me like an exotic fruit.

Like an exotic fruit I intended to do six-pack on! The onlookers moved even further back, clutching at the bar. A terrified old geezer in a postman's uniform suddenly puked into his mailbag with the fear. Or the beer. Or both. I let off a round in his general direction and the sack burst in an explosion of confetti and vomit, spattering the guys on either side of him. They recoiled in disgust like the gun in my fist had.

It was only then that I realised I didn't know what order you were meant to do the six-pack business in. Should I work up one side: foot, kneecap, elbow, or start do both pairs at once but from the top up or down? Were elbows even involved? It was fucking complex. I really should have thought this through beforehand. But it was too late now! So I just shot him in the right foot and his expensive trainer was instantly depreciated. As opposed to being instantly deprecated, which it was too. Fucking shithouse apology for a shoe! He screamed first and then started on the customary howling and gibbering. When I shot him in the other foot great gobbets of blood and bone fragments splodged up onto The Stripper who was by the bar. I watched transfixed as her fingers moved downward to remove a bloody chunk from her neither regions. The chunk was discarded but as she tried to wipe the blood and gunk off herself she only ended up spreading it around, inadvertently arousing herself in the process. A finger slipped into the depths of her feminine mystery and she let out a soft moan. I didn't see that coming. She was obviously one of those women who are sexually aroused by extreme gratuitous violence. This could be a match made in Heaven. They didn't grow on trees you know. Suddenly I was distracted as a crazy fuckwit leapt over the bar brandishing a cricket bat like some kind of berserker! I subconsciously let off another round and it shattered the bat. Huge willow splinters erupted in all directions. A couple of especially evil ones lodged in my assailant's eyeballs. "Ieeeeeeaaaaaiiiiiii" he went, like a racist caricature in an 1970s war comic. I noticed also a bundle of spikes sticking out of his arse-cheeks, and as he hit the deck I wondered at the contortion he must have to performed to make this possible, and how it was inconceivable it should have passed unmentioned in the narrative.

Just then The Stripper grunted, she was still digitally remasterbating as she leaned back on the bar. With her spare hand she manipulated the pert antenna of her starboard hemisphere, eyes closed, lips pouted, standard operational procedure as her climax impended. The guy I was six-packing had fainted, and I realised I was holding him up by his ridiculous hairstyle. The place had pretty much emptied now except for him and her and the guy clutching his eyes and trying to cry like a little girl but failing miserably in his terrible agony. It struck me as ironic that it was his colleague that I had previously regaled with the Oedipal Pejorative.

"GET ON," SHE BARKED, PULLING SOME WIRY SHIT
FROM UNDER THE HANDLEBARS AND FIDDLING WITH IT.

I felt a tug at my sleeve and spun round. It was The Stripper.

"We gotta get out of this place," she went, quoting Cynthia Weil appositely.

"Uh… good idea," I heard myself go.

She pulled me to the door and paused at the coat-rack to pull on a see-thru P VC raincoat and pick up her tankard of takings. I held the door for her chivalrously and the daylight burst in on her and her amazing arse. There was a lime-green Vespa directly outside the pub. She hitched up her mac and threw her leg over.

"Get on," she barked, pulling some wiry shit from under the handlebars and fiddling with it. I got on be-hind her, making sure I straddled the scooter man-fully as it all looked a bit effeminate to me. I heard a bellow from the pub and the doors flew open again. Although I should have been focussing on matters closer to home, I noticed then that the pub was called "The Cock in Hand". Meanwhile the bloke with the eyes thing blumbered outward. He screamed again as the bright sunlight assailed his shredded seeing-bulbs. Then the machine started and she kicked up the kick-stand and off we sped, quite slowly on account of the thing being powered by a motor less powerful than a lot of spin-dryers have but still quick enough to out-run a blinded cunt anyway. Anyway, as the poor gee-zer lunged at us he fell under a street sweeping van that had been bearing down on us washing the kerb stones. The fucking thing was fucking noisy enough.

I'd always thought that the blind were meant to have better hearing to make up for it but that obviously wasn't the case here. The last we saw in the rear-view he was vanishing being sucked feet-first into the spinning brushes. It just wasn't his day.

22:05:1965

Given their contemporaneous origins and similar demographic penetration, it comes as no surprise that the Beatles have been referenced in *Dr Who* more often than any other popular cultural phenomena.

Both of these British icons have spawned world-wide industries of merchandise and analysis, and both tropes were instrumental in bringing "scholarship" of popular culture into academic institutions in a transparent bid to divert efforts away from real-world social phenomena.

The first documented intersection of the two tropes occurred in the first episode of *The Chase*, broadcast 22 May 1965, starring William Hartnell as the First Doctor, known as One to hard-line Whovians. Viewing from the year 1996, a clip of The Beatles singing "Ticket to Ride" (from the 15 April 1965 episode of *Top of the Pops*) is seen on a Time-Space Visualiser, and the Doctor's assistant, Vicki, who is apparently from the 25th century, refers to them as classical music and presciently refers to a museum in Liverpool, dedicated to them in her time. In "reality" the first Beatles museum opened in Liverpool in 1981.

DALEKSPLOITATION TOP 10

1	**I'm Gonna Spend My Christmas With A Dalek** . . . . The Go-Go's	**1964**
2	**Landing of the Daleks** . . . . The Earthlings	**1965**
3	**Dance of the Daleks** . . . . Jack Dorsey Orchestra	**1965**
4	**Who is the Doctor?** . . . . Jon Pertwee	**1972**
5	**I Am a Dalek** . . . . The Art Attacks	**1978**
6	**Tom Baker** . . . . The Human League	**1981**
7	**Doctor in Distress** . . . . Who Cares	**1985**
9	**Doctorin' the Tardis** . . . . The Timelords	**1988**
9	**Negro Necro Nekros** . . . . Dälek	**1998**
10	**Dr Who on Holiday** . . . . Dean Gray	**2005**

The programme producers' original idea had been to have a brief cameo appearance by the actual group, made up to appear elderly and performing at a 1996 theme park but Beatles manager Brian Epstein vetoed the stupid idea. This decision lends retrospective verisimilitude to the show since the band had broken up in 1970 and John Lennon had been murdered by 1980 making that postulated performance seem unlikely.

The footage used for the broadcast is the only known surviving footage of the Beatles on *Top of the Pops*, the original tapes of their appearances having been wiped by the BBC alongside many early episodes of *Dr Who*. Given the clip's miraculous survival, it is ironic that licencing restrictions now require the excision of the clip from most retail versions of the show.

A DOLL'S HOUSE

We sped through the afternoon streets in the sunlight, weaving hazardously in and out of traffic. Scattering pedestrians. Cutting up traffic. Doing all sorts of illegal shit but nobody cares since its only traffic offences and its not like anybody could get hurt. It wasn't an eventful trip. We ended up in an immensely wealthy part of town and all the houses looked like wedding cakes only much bigger and with doors and windows stuck into the icing. Lots of them had massive iron gates with slobbering dogs behind guarding them, so that was realistic.

We pulled up at the gatepost of an arbitrary one of them and the chick held up her wrist to a metal thing on it. Somewhere a fuck-off big relay threw and the gates started to grind open sideways, not like the piss-weak ones that just swing inwards. That was interesting because I had wondered were she kept her keys when she was fiddling the ignition. Like I said, her raincoat was clear vinyl so I could see everything but I couldn't see any keys. We put-putted up to the door of the mansion. There were big roman columns and a bell-pull thing that I thought she was going for. But instead, she lifted the empty plant pot that was beside the door and took the key from underneath it.

I followed her down the hallway. It was pretty dark but I could make out that is was way way swanky. There were oil paintings on the wall and ornaments made of that really pricey china that sort of rings even if you just walk past it with the vibration. It was so quiet that I could hear her hair brushing against the vinyl of her raincoat. As my eyes adjusted to the dark I could make out her luminous buttocks describing a precise Lissajous curve as she sashayed down the corridor. Did I mention about the raincoat being completely see-through?

We went into a room off the end of the hall and she put on a light. It was done out like a Radley Metzger film set. Everything white and curvy with black and white tiles and chrome and glass and leopard-skin. On one wall hung a copy of my favourite painting which was also the only one I could recognise by sight. It was of a beach with a naked chick sitting on the sand and a bloke coming out of the water in a kind of swan outfit.

"Pearson's *Wings of Love*. That's the original," went The Stripper, reading my thoughts disconcertingly with the first words she had spoken since the last ones. She went over to a bar in the corner and pointed at a huge leather sofa that was bigger than all the furniture in my house put together, even if you threw in white-goods, even if white-goods are hard to throw. I sat

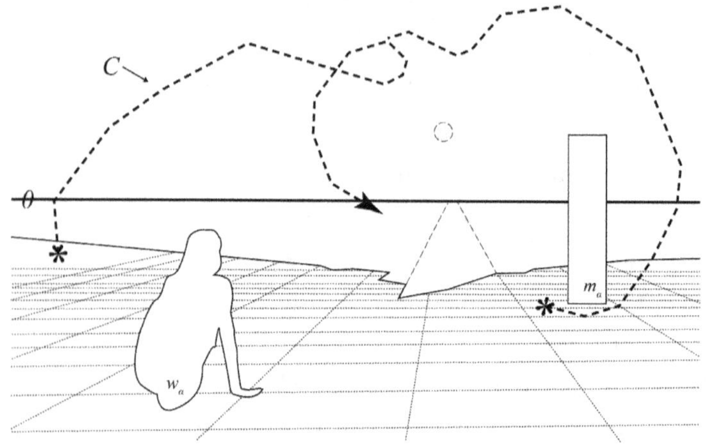

down and the chair made a loud farting noise. Maybe I had a sense of deja vu, or maybe not...

"Blended scotch and chinotto," she went. It wasn't a question.

"In a pint glass. Yes. You've done your homework."

"Oh, it's not due in till Tuesday," she went, humorously bringing over my drink. "Now, you will do me the favour of choosing some music whilst I excuse myself for a moment."

As she got up she pushed a button on some kind of box that was on the coffee table and a rack rose out of the arm of the sofa. It was full of those newfangled Compact Disk things. I pulled out the first one to hand. It took me a while to get the weird jewellery box thing open and then I had to extract the disc from the tray. Obviously, there was a knack. I pushed the disc into a convenient slot and suddenly got blasted

with the unmistakable brain-mangling feedback in-
tro to The Creation doing "Making Time". I looked at
the case. It was a compilation of old sixties tunes but
it didn't have a name on the front. Still it was pleas-
ingly psychedelic and I recognised some of the names
like The Move and Pretty Things, and The Small Fac-
es of course. It was on a label I'd never heard of and
had an address in LA on the back in print that was
small enough so I couldn't make out the exact year
of copyright, only that it started with a number two
so it was obviously a misprint. That was odd. Where
labels were concerned it was known that the smaller
the print the more care they took. They didn't care so
much about the name of the group or the record. That
sort of lack of attention to detail could only mean one
thing. Bootlegs! I put my hand on my piece. My gun,
that is.

22:11:1968

The year of 1968 saw an unprecedented wave of civil unrest
in lots of countries, notably France, Czechoslovakia, West
Germany, Northern Ireland, Brazil, Mexico and the USA. The
month of May in Paris is commonly viewed as the most pho-
togenic youth revolt of the 1960s. The City of Light was in
flames. The Parisian lads had obviously got envious of the
girls wigging out over the Beatles when they had played three
weeks at The Olympia with Sylvie Vartan four years before
so they conjured up their own, testosterone-fuelled, uprising.

In response to the Paris upheavals, the Beatles converged on Kinfaus, George Harrison's palace in Escher, Surrey, to record demos for what would become their ninth LP, officially entitled *The Beatles* but better known as *The White Album*.

The LP kicks off with *Back in the USSR* as if you didn't know—a tune which has been blamed by some for the collapse of the Soviet Union—and it climaxes with the sonic assault of *Revolution 9*, widely considered the longest and worst tune in the Beatles canon… assuming it is a tune.

Many reasons have been postulated for the adoption of 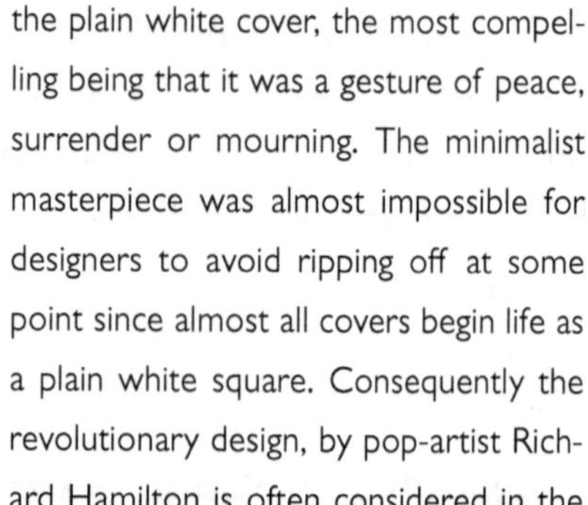 the plain white cover, the most compelling being that it was a gesture of peace, surrender or mourning. The minimalist masterpiece was almost impossible for designers to avoid ripping off at some point since almost all covers begin life as a plain white square. Consequently the revolutionary design, by pop-artist Richard Hamilton is often considered in the public domain. That was just as well since it was directly appropriated eight months later by TMOQ Records when they issued the Bob Dylan recordings that became known as *The Great White Wonder*, widely regarded as the first bootleg LP.

Upon its release on 22 November 1968 (five years to the day since JFK's killing) *The Beatles* received mixed reviews from music critics but, coming more than a year after their last LP and soon after the opening of the *Yellow Submarine* film, the album was huge commercial success, especially in the USA.

Despite the accolades, Few Beatles fans took their proclivities quite as far as Charles Manson, who persuaded members of his entourage that the album was an apocalyptic message predicting a prolonged race war and justified the murder of wealthy people. Manson's alleged "Helter Skelter" hypothesis was a hybrid of the Beatles' mid-period canon and The Book of Revelation, and has been documented in dozens of books. In a nutshell, The Beatles (i.e. the locusts from The Book of Revelation) are harbingers of an apocalyptic conflict between people of different skin-tones. Several of Manson's followers, and he himself, were convicted following some murders starting in mid-1969. It was claimed that the murders had been committed to inspire radicals to more violent styles of activism and to imminentise the eschaton.

It was not until the late ninteteen-eighties that Manson would definitively clarify his role in events, stating:

Do you feel blame? Are you mad? Uh, do you feel like wolf kabob Roth vantage? Gefrannis booj pooch boo jujube; bear-ramage. Jigiji geeji geeja geeble Google. Begep flagaggle vaggle veditch-waggle bagga?

TEAM BUILDING EXERCISE

The old smut pedlar had been a computer whizz in the 1970s. You couldn't call him a hacker since he'd stopped been a hacker before the term was coined. As a childhood maths prodigy and all-county Scrabble champ, he'd easily landed a prime assignment one day back in the sixties or seventies when his dad got a call from a top boffin about a secret research program where they could put his talents to the public good and he could avoid the tedium of going to university just to have it rubber-stamp his already mad skillz. As it happened, The Unit was housed in three tar-paper shacks in a secret shanty town in a paddock adjoining a prestigious university. This was the palaeolithic era of computing when the machines were mainframes the size of big rooms: interconnected steel cabinets painted duck egg blue or institutional grey and some-times a dark green almost khaki if the equipment was ex-M OD. Sometimes the wind would rip through the tar-paper walls of the machine shack and if the rain got in there be a sudden shower of orange sparks and all the lights and everything would go out. Obviously, you'd lose all your code. There were no UP S's in those days.

Inspired by Joseph Weizenbaum's program "Eliza", which simulated nondirective psychotherapy, the pro-grammers were working on computer modelling of what they used to call "mental" "illnesses". The Unit had to be top secret and was concealed from the at-tentions of pharmaceutical companies who had a vest-ed interest in suppressing their research to preserve their markets. Despite their precautions The Unit was subverted at every official turn.

Quickly, the Hacker found celebrity with his razor sharp insights into the alternative mindsets that were being monetised as mental illnesses. After his first briefing, he'd been told to familiarise himself with the equipment, but gone away and churned out a catatonia simulator written in the then new and exotic dialect of BASIC. Later, he surpassed himself and earned the esteem of his colleagues with a simple function that could be added to any programme to mimic the effects of coprolalia, later codified as Tourette's Syndrome. The function worked by piping all standard output through a filter that would periodically add extra expletives or apparently random outbursts or sometimes just crash the machine.

Things started to go pear-shaped when some members of the team started experimenting with drugs the better understand the altered states that they were trying to model. The effects of marijuana could be approximated by stealing machine cycles to run unnecessary high-demand routines that would do nothing but garble the output in only occasionally entertaining ways.

He'd been fired without ceremony after a Unit exercise in the wilds of Dartmoor. Six colleagues and his immediate superior were packed into a Transit sitting in the car park in the belting rain when he jumped suddenly out of the van and stripped stark naked then started running in circles around it waving a convenient hatchet over his head and screaming "I KNOW EXACTLY WHAT I'M DOING!!!" over and over again. To be fair everyone was tripping their tits off.

It was funny at the time but a bit embarrassing in hindsight so he never did it again.

The next time he showed up for work all the huts had been torn down and there was only dead brown grass to tell him that he'd found the right place but it was too late and now it was the wrong place. He didn't know what to do next so he went and signed on the dole and spent a couple of weeks reading SF anthologies in bookshops around town. Soon enough he ran into someone down the pub who worked in a bookshop and they recognised him so they offered him a job.

The Beatles had split by the end of 1970 just after George released his solo debut triple-LP *All Things Must Pass*. It was a triple-album since John and Paul compositions dominated Beatles LPs and so George had heaps of tunes saved up. On 10 February 1971, Bright Tunes, a financially-ailing US music publisher, filed suit against his song "My Sweet Lord" for alleged copyright infringement against "He's So Fine" by the Chiffons, written by the late Ronnie Mack.

Harrison's manager, Allen Klein, entered into negotiations with Bright Tunes to try and resolve the issue by offering to buy the publisher's entire catalogue but no settlement could be reached before the company was forced into receivership.

1 **Folsom Prison Blues** ...Johnny Cash vs Gordon Jenkins **1968**

2 **My Sweet Lord**........ George Harrison vs The Chiffons **1970**

3 **Whole Lotta Love** ......Led Zeppelin vs. Muddy Waters **1969**

4 **Ghostbusters**... Ray Parker Jr. vs Huey Lewis & the News **1984**

5 **The Old Man Down the Road**
...........John Fogerty vs Creedence Clearwater Revival **1985**

6 **Ice Ice Baby** ....Vanilla Ice vs Queen & Bowie **1990**

7 **Whatever**........................ Oasis vs. The Rutles **1994**

8 **Shakermaker** .... Oasis vs. The New Seekers **1994**

9 **Connection** .... Elastica vs. Wire **1994**

10 **Bittersweet Symphony**..... Verve vs The Rolling Stones **1997**

In September 1976 the court found that Harrison had "subconsciously" copied the earlier tune, since he admitted to having been aware of the prior recording. The judge ordered Harrison to pay more than us$1.5 million but while that figure was being argued Klein succeeded in purchasing the rights so that Harrison would have to pay him instead. It was one of the longest running legal battles ever to be litigated in the us and matters would not finally be concluded until March 1998.

The ruling was a personal blow for Harrison who admitted he was too unsettled by the experience to write anything new for some time afterwards. The precedent had also seen Little Richard claim for breach of copyright in a track recorded by the Beatles on their *Beatles for Sale* album. As a result of the Bright Tunes case's astronomical legal expenses to both sides, with no clear winner, subsequent charges of plagiarism in the music industry have often resulted in a policy of swift settlement, ostensibly to limit damage to an artist's "credibility".

One odd outcome of these precedents was that in 1985 John Fogerty was accused by his former label of plagiarising his own tune "Run Through the Jungle" which had been recorded by his former group Creedence Clearwater Revival. Both tunes were played in court, Fogerty was cleared and promptly counter-sued for unpaid royalties. The case went to the Supreme Court, which is no relation to the Motown combo. Most of our sensory impressions are now of media rather than of the natural world. It's impossible to listen to every record just to try and avoid duplicating one, so how can this be avoided? An industry has grown to develop algorithms for melodic similarity. Implementations of these can automate the process of avoiding or detecting similarity. What could possibly go wrong?

BACKWARDS MASKING

By the time The Eyes had got to "When The Night Falls", the skyclad fox had re-entered the room, newly showered and towelling her tresses.

"What's the most unusual place you've had sex?" She asked.

"Eastbourne!" I answered without thinking.

"What's unusual about that?"

"It was just the once." I went, eager to get to the bottom of her, "How did you get into this line of work?"

"I wanted to be a prostitute but I disapproved of pimping. Prostitution might be the oldest profession but pimping wasn't far behind."

"Yeah. It's weird. A 'pro' used to mean a prostitute but now it means a professional but 'turning pro' still means the same thing… "

"A pimp's first job is to keep other pimps away from the girl, which of course renders all pimps mutually redundant. Their strictest sanctions are reserved not for unpaying punters but for the girls who give themselves away for free. That's not because of the lost revenue, it's the demarcation. Gouging punters is their job. Woe betide the whore who falls in love."

"All human creative endeavour originated in sexual display. Striptease was the first artform, long before language. All dance is just a coy form of exotic dancing, which itself predates clothing. The animal kingdom provides many precedents."

"I always said that Sir David Attenborough was a bigger perv than Paul Raymond. So who are you working for now?"

"Can't you tell from my uniform yet?" She went, running her shapely fingers all over her shapely thingies, "the livery of the human species. Always different, always the same. All other uniforms must be worn over the skin, which is analogous to the ordering of subordinate flags, for instance."

"Is that why strippers often favour uniforms? Nurses. Policewomen. French maids. Stewardesses?"

"But paradoxically, our lingerie tends to the exotic. Institutional underwear is favoured for ironic, and uh specialised, tastes."

"The occult infrastructure of the female form. At the next level down, the various types of lingerie are uniforms in themselves. Most brands are aligned with minor celebrities and TV has-beens. Often punters just come right out and wear the brand of a globalised corporation. They are conscripting us into their uniforms from the inside out.

"But even so, it doesn't matter, since we are all spies wearing our true colours underneath, so ultimately serving a higher power... our common humanity!"

"That's why witches are always nude in those seventies films then?"

"Quite. You're very observant."

She came over and took a swig from my drink, finishing it.

"I'm just going to slip into something more uncomfortable," she went, going out but this time leaving the door open. I wondered why she'd turned bashful but then I realised how terribly drafty it was. I could clock her in the other room, silhouetted in the doorway. The Fleur de Lys came on and I could hear her as she bumped and ground to the heavy garage slop. I tried to crank up the volume but pushed the wrong button and the disc started spinning in reverse. It sounded twice as cool. I looked to see if there was a way to speed it up too but couldn't figure it.

That was strange. She had got a pair of very briefs from somewhere which she sort of rubbed over herself before slowly easing them on and teasing them up. Then she fiddled with the elastic and all that, rubbing her exciting parts and pouting and stuff. Then she started running her hands up her smooth curves and switched her attention to her fantastic overt assets. Did I mention her overt assets? They were pretty good ones. Reaching over she grabbed a brassiere from wherever she'd got the scanty panties from and quickly clutched it to her, but she didn't put it on straightaway. Her pert nipples stood proudly like twin radio masts on two adjacent hills. I expect that's how they get stereo. She jiggled the Büstenhalter around getting it to fit right exactly before reaching round and fastening it with a huge amount of difficulty. Reaching back, she caressed her lonely domes and corrupt curves through the lacy fabric. The stockings came next. She rolled them on very slowly. Her legs seemed to go on forever. A surprisingly modest skirt ash-grey, languidly slidden over her buttocks and zipped, and then the same with the formal blouse then a matching military-style blouson jacket, and lastly some of those elbow-length gloves that that Spanish pervert Jesus

Franco had been so fond of. By then she was dressed and came back out to the lounge. I gave her a rousing round of applause to be polite. Up closer I noticed her dress was on some kind of mohair fabric. The grey wool teased out to such a length that you couldn't tell exactly where the environment ended and she began. The interstitial area formed a luminous aura when she walked in front of the lamp like the sky on an alien world.

05:1973

Although preceded by avant-garde and comedic precedents, modern remixing—the recombination of existing musical components to create a new version—is widely considered to have its roots in the dancehall culture of late-sixties/early-seventies Jamaica. The fluid evolution of local music that had morphed mento to ska to rocksteady to reggae was embraced by local music producers who deconstructed tracks into versions suitable for toasting, the local practise of DJs singing or chanting over the top of records at sound system parties. Innovative producers and engineers like King Tubby and Lee "Scratch" Perry popularized stripped-down instrumental mixes (known as "versions") of reggae tunes. At first they simply dropped the vocal tracks, but soon more sophisticated effects were created, dropping individual tracks in and out of the mix, isolating and repeating hooks, and adding various effects like echo, reverberation and delay.

In May 1973, Lee "Scratch" Perry, undoubtedly the greatest ever innovator of recording, remade Leo Graham's "News Splash" as "Station Underground News", dropping in a taped sample of the Chi-Lites "(For God's Sake) Give More Power to the People" from 1971. This was the earliest known instance of a beat-matched sample from a different song being used in a recording.

By the mid-1970s, dub culture had arrived in the Bronx via Caribbean immigrants such as Jamaican DJ Kool Herc and Barbados-born Grandmaster Flash. Sound-systems were translated into block parties where DJs played soul and funk records in place of reggae, and toasting became rapping, substituting jive-talk for patois. In Jamaica DJs had access to studios for their remixing into dub versions, but in NYC it had to be done on the fly, and because the percussive breaks in funk, soul and disco records were generally short, Herc and other DJs began using two turntables to extend the breaks. Cutting (alternating between duplicate copies of the same record) and scratching (manually moving the vinyl record beneath the turntable needle) became part of the emerging culture known as Hip-Hop. Turntablist techniques—such as scratching (attributed to Grand Wizzard Theodore), beat mixing and/or matching, and beat juggling—eventually developed along with the breaks. The new medium gave a voice to the disenfranchised youth of low socioeconomic demographics and the culture reflected the political realities of their lives.

Caribbean families had settled in the UK since the Windrush docked in 1948 but their music really started permeating working-class areas in the early sixties, finding an audience amongst mods and subsequently skinheads and punks. By the eighties reggae had morphed into jungle, which spawned dubstep. Its cultural impact was such that, by the 21st century, Caribbean patois was the lingua franca of youth of all epidermal patinas.

The rapid developments in Jamaican music were arguably attributable to the absence of restrictive legislation. Overseas white-owned corporate labels had made a racist practise of ignoring local artists, and local record labels had always been liberal when it came to appropriation, themselves lacking funds or framework for litigation. Covers, remakes and versions of songs paid no heed to European-derived notions of property since musical recordings were not copyrightable. Disputes of ownership usually concerned absence of royalties rather than licensing and were not settled in court but in the street with fists, ratchets and firearms. Given the lawlessness of the island there were higher priorities than oxymorons such as intellectual property. The sufferers' daily struggle for survival gave them a profound insight into such spurious constructs. It wasn't until 1993 that Jamaica's Copyright Act came into effect and 1996 when the Jamaica Music Society (otherwise known as The JAMMS) was instituted.

Now the doomed and annoying fuckementarian went to the ye shoppe in ye parke to get ye black tea and perhaps ye scone. A studenty-looking bloke with a beard and a tape recorder and microphone was prodding bushes nearby and trying to get sounds of birdsong or maybe people copulating but it was a bit early for that.

He gave up on the bushes and got a bag from his pocket and started tossing small pinches of birdseed around to attract the pigeons for some arcane reason. The birds seemed unimpressed by his equipment and ran off when he brandished his oversized microphone at them. But one bird went against the tide! Was it hungrier or braver or more stupid? We'll probably never know. It waddled up cautiously and commenced pecking the tasty grains. It took a minute for the penny to drop but its comrades soon noticed and tried to discourage the scab. Then, as several, they descended on him and tried to drive him off. They should have known that if he'd been mad enough to try it in the first place he must be desperate enough to fight for it now but no. It all escalated horribly and before you knew it they were pecking the poor little blighter's head in. It was like a horrible perversion of that Edgar Broughton banger "Evening Over Rooftops" off of *The Meat Album*.

LAST THING HE SAW THEY WERE PECKING
THE POOR FUCKER'S EYES OUT.

Mind you, the bloke with the tape recorder oggled the horrible spectacle aghast and rooted to the spot. Then suddenly he realised what he'd started and dove in waving his arms and trying to drive off the angry birds. The birds had done their job well and the scab pigeon was twitching in his death agonies. Or maybe birds are like fish and didn't actually feel pain. I'm not a fucking expert. Drunk with avian gore and curious to sample the variety of a new species they descended like harbingers of doom on the pitiful field-recordist. Pretty soon he was screaming and crying and flailing around like a mad bastard as the militant birds showed him what for! They were shredding his beard! It was a shit beard in the first place. Well, it turns out that people bleed even easier than birds and sooner or later one was gonna hit an artery. It was going to turn ugly! But by now our eroticist protagonist had finished his scone and tea and was losing interest so he missed the end. Last thing he saw they were pecking the poor fucker's eyes out. Fucking hell! Who'd want to work in a Casualty Department?

THE HOUSE WAS RIGGED

Just then I remembered that I'd forgotten to ask The Stripper about the bootleg CD but she kicked off on her shtick before I got the chance.

"I represent the interests of a heavily resourced secret global organisation," she began promisingly. "For thirty-odd years we've been investigating various aspects of 'reality' and have managed to cobble together a functioning world-view from the best bits of other philosophies and theologies. Our founder, whom for obvious reasons I cannot name, set up this division in 1966 for the primary purpose of procuring his mistresses. After he ceased operations in Orthogonal Time we had to redefine our role and we decided that serious research into this area was long overdue. We want you to work with us, to help us discover the answer to a deceptively modest question."

"Like I give a fuck?" I went, I wasn't swallowing none of that shit. Deja vu or not.

There was an uncomfortable pause, but not as bad as all that.

"Why do you do what you do?" She went, unprompted.

"I wish I knew."

"Don't you know?"

"I don't know."

"You don't know whether you know or not?"

"No."

"Don't you mean 'yes'?"

"I don't know."

"You don't know if you mean you don't know whether you know or not?"

"I know."

"Would you like to?"

"Sometimes I think I know but other times I think I don't know. And sometimes I feel like I know but I don't actually think I do. Other times I feel like I know whether I think I do know or not but that never lasts long."

"Wouldn't you like to know?"

"More than anything."

"Anything?" She moved closer and I wondered if things were perhaps about to turn sexy.

"Anything except why my Glock—if it is a Glock—keeps discharging accidentally."

"Oh that's easy…" went the knowledgeable exotic dancer, "Everyone has 'I don't know why I did that' moments all the time. These actions are just the continuum adjusting itself to temporal paradoxes due to future time travel. The moments when you lack so-called 'free will'. Some people like to postulate a secret cabal of "Timewasters" hunting down and killing the paradoxes but those are just the ravings of opportunists with vested interests. No disrespect… I'm a fan. Obviously, things that happen quickly are the most dangerous because they're over before you realise they've happened. Watch out for those."

"Is that meant to be some kind of denouement? That explains a lot of things."

"Look… I'll show you!" She went, cryptically, and she got up and went over to the bookshelf to take down a hefty leather-bound volume and open it. There must have been some kind of remote control inside because she fiddled with it and the bookcase slid smoothly sideways with a horrible loud grinding sound. There was a gleaming white fluorescent wave of light washed over us and we walked towards it…

1984

If the anarchic copyright regime in Jamaica had a polar opposite it might be found in the Soviet Union. Following the October Revolution the first copyright law was passed in 1925

and went through several major revisions during its existence. The Soviet Union lacked any international copyright relations until an agreement with Hungary in 1967 but in 1973 the USSR then joined the Universal Copyright Convention and established copyright relations with Western countries. More bilateral treaties followed until in 1989 the government announced its intention to join the Berne Convention.

There was a lively music scene throughout the history of the Soviet Union as the polymorphic output of the state record label Melodiya attests. Professional musicians were esteemed members of the society and well looked after but the situation for amateurs was different. The strict laws against individuals engaging in any private business forbade musicians from charging admission to shows or from selling recordings of their music. In response the magnitizdat phenomena arose. This was the process of re-copying and self-distributing live audio tape recordings that were not available commercially, similar to Western bootlegs except that these releases were generally sanctioned by the performers. Magnitizdat was less risky than publishing unofficial literature via samizdat since anyone in the USSR was permitted to own a tape recorder while paper duplication equipment was more strictly controlled.

After the founding of the Leningrad Rock Club in 1981, there was an explosion of popular music in the USSR as groups emerged from the underground into the mainstream. The two most successful groups to break through were Akvarium, led by Boris Grebinshikov, and Kino, led by Viktor Tsoi, who were both fortunate to record in the West. The Rock Club was distrusted by many musicians and fans as it was an official institution and was believed to be monitored by the KGB. More radical bands like Televizor were not allowed to play there so an underground movement continued to exist.

With limited access to Western equipment and Soviet technology in short supply the USSR developed a thriving DIY electronics and hi-fi scene and the ingenuity of the Soviet musicians was boundless. Maybe the most spectacular example was supplied by **«Братья по разуму»** (Brothers In Mind). The group was founded in 1983 by Vladimir "Vova Blue" Emelev and Igor "Gosha Ryzhiy" Shaposhnikov in the secret scientific city of Chelyabinsk-70. In 1984, the group recorded their debut album *88A* by splicing fragments of tapes of Western records and overdubbing their vocals. It is believed that this was the first Soviet album to use samples. The following year the group released several more albums on magnitizdat: *Игра Синих Лампочек* (Game of Blue Lights,

1985), *Молчать!* (Be Silent!, 1985), *Хали-Гали* (Hully-Gul-ly, 1985), *Ну как не запеть* (How Not To Sing, 1986).

After a couple of years doing military service Vladimir moved to Moscow (later Igor joined him) where he revived the group and started giving live concerts eventually supporting Sonic Youth when they played in Moscow in 1989.

Predating The Justified Ancients of Mu Mu's *1987* by a few years, the Brothers' work sounds at least as revolutionary—even if you don't understand any of the words.

STRANGE BEDFELLOW

The old pornœologist looked at his watch. It was time for bed. He always resented being awake and regarded it as a necessary inconvenience of existence like eating or going to the toilet or reproducing sexually. Chance would be a fine thing. He thought that the most important times of your life were spent asleep, dreaming and communing with the infinite. He was skilled in lucid dreaming and astral projection and enjoyed the unlimited power that he could exercise without repercussion in the universe of his unconscious.

You know about the bedside table by now… the actual bed itself wasn't half as interesting. The old hack didn't have any heating in his house so he had to sleep between alternating sheets of tinfoil and woollen blankets from the Salvation Army to keep warm. This had the effect of turning his bed into a kind of orgone accumulator which might explain why his vices and indolence hadn't killed him by now.

Above the headboard like a figurehead was tacked an old postcard of the Angel of the Promenade that used to look over him as he slept on the beach all through the cold night if he was too pissed to make it all the way home. It was the last thing he looked at every night and her image burned into his knack-ered retina and stayed there until he finally fell asleep. Just so long as he didn't open his eyes. Sometimes she would still be hovering there while he dreamed and he would try and work her into the narrative with varying degrees of success.

It was like a wise old head had told him once. The trick wasn't going as far out as you possibly could. It was all about being able to make it back home after-wards so you could file your report. When it came to an expedition, some people were preoccupied with getting home afterwards and some didn't give a fuck where they crashed anyway. Even if they had homes to go to. But some poor souls vacillated and didn't know where to draw the line and tried to make it back to where they thought they could sleep safely and snugly but perished on the way before they got there. Think Jack Kerouac at the side of the track all frozen and black. He never made it back. There's your proof. There's scores of thousands just the same. It could have been him a hundred times over more or less. He wasn't counting. He'd just liked sleeping there because if he got stabbed to death on the beach in the night at least he'd have an impressive headstone.

Underneath the relative luxury of his current bed he kept his stash of massively rare vintage porn paperbacks and all his notes and research from over the years. Pages were spilling out messily. The old writer was always terrified of pissing the bed in the night and spoiling it all. Every fucking beer was like spinning the chamber like a game of Russian Roulette except with a cock instead of a gun and piss instead of bullets. I expect that would hurt your bollocks. Moving on…

12:03:1987

The Hit Parade can be viewed as a primitive albeit uninteresting instrument intended to conflate the commercial potential of cultural phenomena with its intrinsic aesthetic value, assuming it had some.

In March 1987 the business and propagandist methods of the Military Entertainment Complex in the UK conspired to manufacture a craze for cover versions and reissues of classic tunes leading to a bizarre temporal gridlock of the Hit Parade.

Was this a bumbling experiment in social engineering an attempt to scramble the temporal fixture of the population of England? We may never know….

What we do know is that the ninth day of this month saw the release of a

CHART OF DARKNESS

1	**Everything I Own**	Boy George **1972**
2	**I Get the Sweetest Feeling**	Jackie Wilson **1968**
3	**Live It Up**	Mental as Anything **1984**
4	**The Great Pretender**	Freddie Mercury **1955**
5	**Stand by Me**	Ben E. King **1960**
6	**Respectable**	Mel & Kim **1987**
7	**When a Man Loves a Woman**	Percy Sledge **1966**
8	**Crush on You**	Jets **1985**
9	**Male Stripper**	Man 2 Man Meets Man Parrish **1986**
10	**Running in the Family**	Level 42 **1987**

mysterious one-sided white label promo 500 only limited edition 12" single. This record was the original release of The Justified Ancients of Mu Mu's "All You Need Is Love"—unrelated to the homonomous Beatles tune other than in title, spirit and its short introductory sample. Because it featured lots of unauthorised sampling the record was denied commercial distribution. The JAMMs modified some of the samples and reissued the record in May. They used the income to produce the most erudite evocation of the state of the nation in their annonynmous (sic) debut album.

Recorded for the most part on an Apple II computer and intended for limited underground circulation, the creators, soon outed as Bill Drummond and Jimmy Cauty, didn't bother with copyright clearances.

Unfortunately the record was so well-reviewed in the major British music publications that it came to the attention of the management of Swedish pop group ABBA. The JAMMs had sampled large portions of "Dancing Queen" on their track "The Queen and I". A showdown with ABBA and the Mechanical Copyright Protection Society followed. *1987* was forcibly withdrawn from sale and The JAMMs were ordered to deliver up the master tape, mothers, stampers and any other parts commensurate with manufacture of the record.

Little did the Reactionary Forces twig that the damage was done. Like a malignant meme, the disc would permeate the noosphere and a hundred flowers bloom. The subtitle "What the Fuck is Going on?" would become an epithet of THE INTERNET, abbreviated as "WTF?"

In response, the protagonists would rebrand themselves The Timelords and rise like an archaeopteryx from the ashes to score a number one hit with "Doctorin' the Tardis", a bizarre crasis of the *Dr Who* theme tune with Gary Glitter and The Sweet. Drummond described the abomination as

"probably the most nauseating record in the world". For this release, the duo assumed the identity of Cauty's 1968 Ford Galaxie police car in an obvious reference to *The Blues Brothers*, John Landis's hilarious and groovy masterpiece that postulates musical solidarity as a strategy against white supremacy.

After that, Bill and Jimmy took the name KLF (Kopyright Liberation Front) and went on to have several more #1 hits and to instigate the acid house underground psychedelic renaissance rave scene of the second Summers of Love in both 1988 and 1989.

TIME ISN'T MONEY

The laboratory was trying to hum a Bruce Haack tune and failing in the attempt. It was an unself-conscious kind of humming like when you walk in the fourth floor khazi and the boss is in one of the cubicles and he hasn't heard you come in coz his skull is humming with the resonant frequency. The lab was white too and it looked like an office khazi more than anything else; like all laboratories do to the uninitiated... except there were nautical paintings all over the walls.

"We got the whole shebang as a job lot." The fox elaborated, "Navy surplus. The Organisation has... connections."

"What did you want to show me?" I went. Understandably, I was curious. So much so that I was jumbling my worms up.

"Time," she went.

"How much?"

"A monkey."

"What would I do with a monkey?"

"Sit down," she motioned towards an office chair in the centre of the lab. There was a massive ray-gun

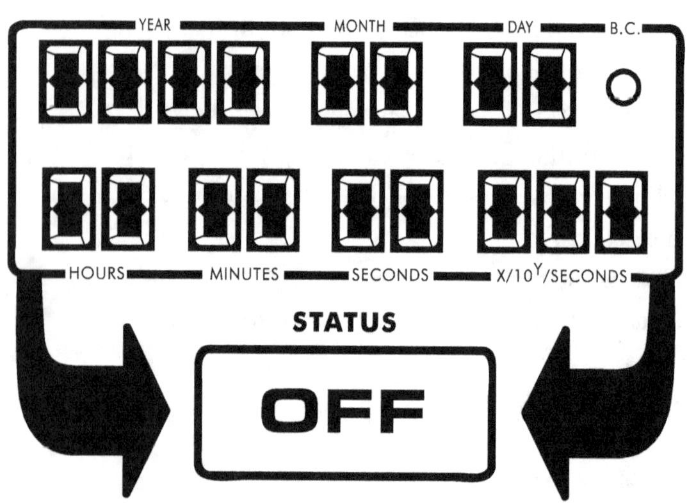

"GIVE ME THAT OLD TIME-REVISION!"

thing like out of a Warner Brothers cartoon pointed at it. It even had the Illudium Q-36 Explosive Space Modulator sticking out of it. I was sure that if I pulled it out it would have ACME CORP written on the side. But that would piss off the fox and we would have to get into a ridiculous chase sequence and kill each other a number of times in surreal and entertaining ways. So I sat down.

A couple of dwarves came in. They were wearing lab coats and carrying clipboards like you'd expect, except they weren't really dwarves. I made that bit up. They were statuesque clones of each other like the women out of that Robert Palmer video. Except they were blonde. Actually, there was a follow-up video where the chicks were blonde anyway so that makes sense. Good.

The erstwhile Stripper got behind the console and threw some switches. They hit the wall with a thudding noise and bits of plaster came off. Then these weird aluminium wrist and ankle restraints came out of the chair and I was strapped in like in a Japanese tentacle sex cartoon. Only there wasn't an octopus handy. But there was still time. At least, I hoped it would keep still.

"What's with all the nautical shit?" I went. Making chit-chat so's I didn't wet myself or burst in even worst ways. Like in those Japanese tentacle sex cartoons.

"We got the whole shebang as a job lot. Navy surplus," she went, attending to various dials and knobs. "I just said that."

"What are the Navy doing with time travel?" I went. I'd twigged this was the time travel caper from the writing on the side of the cannon I just described. On the nose of the Chron-O-Funnel™ itself was a painting of Mae West with a strap-on taking Hitler up the arse like you might see on a WWII bomber but I had no fucking idea what that was all about.

"It makes sense that the Navy would be conducting research. After all, what is to water as mirror is to window? But, as you see, they either abandoned it or got something better. Otherwise they wouldn't have flogged the stuff to us."

"What could be better than time travel?"

"I dunno. Maybe they just decided they liked water better. It's not as wet."

"Or maybe an entirely new branch of the armed forces was formed. And the Navy forced to disband its research."

"It makes sense that the navy would be involved. The sea covers the surface of the globe spanning a two-dimensional surface uniformly. Until this century, the third dimension was not meaningfully accessible to us. With the coming of age of flight, new armed forces, air forces, were created to police this newly exploitable dimension. It follows that a time force would be created if travel through the dimension of time were to be mastered. The Army and Navy competed against each other at the advent of flight. Wouldn't all three branches of the services be competing now?"

Suddenly, annoying voices noisily boist out the tannoy.

"X-Rays."

"Pulse?"

"Pulse normal."

"Breathing steady."

"Electrolytic cream." She started smearing crazy jelly crap on random bits of me. That was good.

"Clamp."

"It looks fine."

"Small probe."

"Pulse 85 increasing."

"Relax!"

"Cream, nurse."

"Right."

"Switch on the cerebral pulsator."

"Give me the electrodes."

"She is introducing the electrodes into the frontal area."

"This is the critical part."

"Pulse?"

"Steady at 89."

"Good. Electrodes in position. I'll take over. She's about to apply the current. One mistake now and…"

I recognised the instructions from an old episode of *Captain Scarlet*. This kind of synchronicity is not

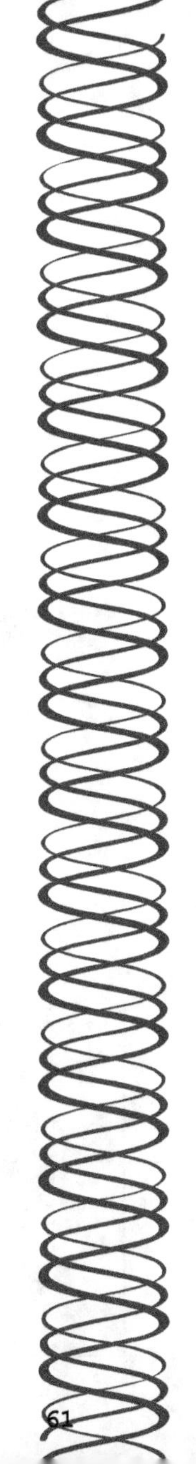

unusual in popular culture and gives secret government agencies like mine nightmares as they try to plug leaks that don't exist. Strangely, it is more usually the case that works of extreme imagination, like the aforementioned Gerry and Sylvia Anderson project, coincide with genuine secret projects. Almost as if the creators are reverse engineering the future. Or maybe just reporting from it. My mind was racing. I was so excited but I didn't even know why yet. WAH! Suddenly everything went completely psychedelic on me. Behold! Now The Funnel starts!!

27:08:1991

By the early nineties, Hip-Hop had become a hugely profitable industry. Following two classic albums, expectations were high for Biz Markie (styled as The Clown Prince of Hip Hop) when he released his third LP, *I Need a Haircut*, in August 1991. Critical reaction was ambivalent and sales were disappointing but the album nevertheless had a profound impact on the development of the genre.

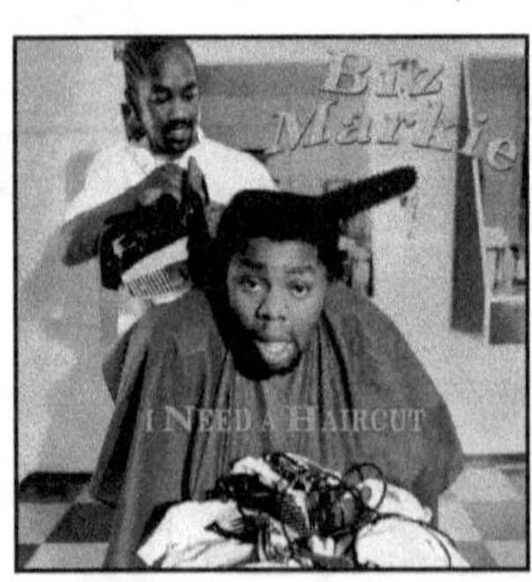

One of the tracks, "Alone Again" featured an uncleared twenty second sample from Gilbert O'Sullivan's maudlin 1972 hit "Alone Again (Naturally)". Unimpressed, O'Sullivan's publishing company brought suit against the label.

Rendering his verdict Judge Kevin Thomas Duffy ignored the nuances of copyright law and likened Biz Markie to a common thief stating "Thou shalt not steal has been an admonition followed since the dawn of civilisation" and issued an injunction against the future distribution of the album and the song. He also referred the case to a district attorney for possible criminal prosecution. Although

Biz never did porridge for his alleged violation of the Seventh Commandment the case set a precedent for seeing unlicensed sampling as a crime. Biz would poke fun at his misfortunes calling his next album *All Samples Cleared!* but his career had been damaged by the publicity and sales of the record suffered accordingly.

As a result of the court case the era of carefree sampling was over and the sound of Hip-Hop music, drawn from combinations of samples from diverse sources, was forced to change. Sample-heavy albums in the vein of Public Enemy's *It Takes a Nation of Millions to Hold Us Back* or the Beastie Boys' *Paul's Boutique* were rammed with literally dozens of samples and would be no longer viable as every sample had to be cleared to avoid legal action. Clearance fees prohibited the use of more than one or two samples for most recordings, with original recording artists sometimes requesting up to 100% of the publishing revenue for use of a single sample.

Many artists continued to sample but retreated into using more and more obscure source material.

These developments hit smaller independent labels disproportionately, but even a group as viable as Public Enemy were unable to issue "Psycho of Greed" on their 2002 *Revolverlution* LP. Built round a sample of the Beatles' song "Tomorrow Never Knows", the clearance fee was so high that the track was pulled from the album.

It is hard for an objective observer to believe that there is not a systematically racist sentiment driving all this. It comes as no surprise that the first popular uprising of the new musical sampling technologies was by Black urban youth… the same sorts of kids who'd invented jazz and rock-n-roll generations back. The Man had tried to suppress those too. After Alcohol Prohibition ended in 1933, funding for the Federal Bureau of Narcotics (now the Drug Enforcement Administration) was reduced dramatically. The FBN's director, Harry J. Anslinger, then became a leading advocate of Marijuana Prohibition. In hearings on the Marijuana Tax Act of 1937, Anslinger testified before Congress saying:

> Marijuana is the most violence causing drug in the history of mankind. Most marijuana smokers are Negroes, Hispanics, Filipinos and entertainers. Their satanic music, jazz and swing result from marijuana usage. This marijuana causes white women to seek sexual relations with Negroes.

Of course, many US states also had laws banning "mixed-race" marriages, some dating from before independence, and many were in effect until as recently as 1967. Thus the Holy Trinity of sex, drugs and rock-n-roll were weaponised into mere attack vectors for systematic racism.

In one important respect, the old spunkmonger was not a total fuck-up since he did possess one of the finest private libraries in the country. He kept it in a lock-up garage nearby that he'd found unlocked once and just taken possession of.

He specialised in English language paperbacks published in Paris. The highlights were from the mid-fifties to the mid-sixties, the heyday of the Olympia Press, but by no means limited to this. He also had a soft spot for Soho typescripts. These were bundles of loose, usually foolscap, sheets, often in the distinctive vivid purple ink of Gestetner duplicating machines. Sometimes they were illustrated with blurred and overexposed photos that were graphically explicit records of congress between generally unattractive couples, both genders generally unnaturally hirsute.

The old writer felt such an affinity for these occult items that when he'd once seen a Gestetner at a boot sale, he'd bought it for a song. Literally. He hadn't got the money for it so he'd pinched the hat of a convenient on-the-nod busker. It didn't have enough silver in it so he'd thrown in the hat itself too. It was an original forties Harris Tweed deerstalker in immaculate condition and obviously nicked recently by the buskie junker. The writer got twenty quid for it from a dealer in ridiculously overpriced retro gear who he'd clocked listening to The Downliners Sect and so he knew he was onto a sure thing.

He'd used the Gestetner to run off copies of manuscripts of porno novels that he'd churn out himself on his Olivetti Lettera 32. An elegant black and cyan machine of Italian extraction. He used the stencil cutting setting which dropped out the red/black ribbon completely and was able to run off as many as twenty copies of each eighty-page manuscript before he'd get fed up. He'd planned to flog these to second-hand book dealers as original manuscripts from the 1950s. But they looked so great and authentic and convincing that he couldn't bear to part with them and he kept every single copy he produced. He got so used to generating these manuscripts that he could do it regardless of his unusual state of consciousness. Some mornings he would wake up and his latest work would be mysteriously finished like in the fairy story about the gnome and the cobblers. This was best of all since he could then have the fun of reading the book as well as writing it.

Titles included: *Jet Sexx, Her Soft Anvil, International Sex Probe, Roughly a Dozen Money Shots!, Tsunami of Jism, Pink Stainless Tail, Mondo Cunt, The Sex Organisation, Arse on Wheels, The Pink and the Grey, XORgasm, Spunk Pirates, The Enormous Hero, Cruel Erotology, My Thighs!, The Story of It, The Bedroom Rooms*. There was even one called *The Hindu Philosophers* and fuck knew where that came from either.

It was a wild ride on the Chron-O-Funnel™. All psychedelic like the end of *Behind The Green Door* (or that Doris Wishman one, what was it? *Satan Was A Lady*) more than *2001*, even though there wasn't any sex in that portentous chocolate-box nonsense. For the unenlightened that means sprawling luminous washes of oil emulsion on vistas of green and purple with disembodied voices piping out of nowhere and then a sudden rushing noise and a stroboscopic refraction that switches on the rods but the cones fire anyway and the synapses burst with flowers summery and the gentle spray in your face as you walk past a fountain with the birdsong and the spray dries instant in the rays of the sun when you hear a laugh behind you and you turn and glimpse a flash out of the corner of your eye you can't make out what she yells but it sounds like your name and you look in her hand because the radiance is too lovely because she is holding a twenty pound note but it isn't The Queen it's the other side. It's some Victorian twat with a beard. Charles Dickens*. His head

---

* Obviously The Bastardizer is mistaken. It was William Shakespeare who appeared on the Bank of England Series D £20 note, in circulation from 9 July 1970 until 19 March 1993. Dickens appeared on the reverse of the Series E £10 note, which was issued on 29 April 1992 and remained in circulation until 31 July 2003. There is no way by which The Bastardizer could have known that fact at the time of his time travel, unless, of course, he'd been into the future some time previously, which he hadn't.

got bigger and bigger and bigger filling my field of vision and all the little etching lines getting resolving themselves and unnatural hues of cyan taking on more human pigments. A quick zoom backwards like that shot of Roy Schneider on the beach in *Jaws* and there I fucking was with the beardy cunt as large as you like on the podium in front of me in some kind of big wood-panelled hall filled with folks, mostly blokes, in period costumes. There was a big diagram of some kind hanging on a screen behind him. Chas was pretty worked up, railing and thumping the podium so that his notes jumped up and he swept them off to swish to the floor in disgust. Then the sound kicked in: "I was about to say that Shakespeare derived some of his plots from old tales and legends in general circulation; but it seems to me, that some of the gentlemen of your craft, at the present day, have shot very far beyond him—"

It was ugly. He was railing away and bits of spit were coming out and sticking in his beard. And he had hair coming out his ears and nose like they did in those days. Then a lanky bastard in a stove-pipe hat jumped up from the front row and did some ejaculating of his own: "You're quite right, sir," he yelled in a weird Yank

Interestingly, the Dickens note was superseded relatively quickly due to its ease of forgery. He was replaced on the note by the even more hirsute Charles Darwin, whose improved beard was harder for forgers, or anyone else for that matter, to duplicate.

accent. "Human intellect, sir, has progressed since his time—is progressing—will progress—"

Chas was having none of it. "Shot beyond him, I mean," he resumed, "in quite another respect, for, whereas he brought within the magic circle of his genius, traditions peculiarly adapted for his purpose, and turned familiar things into constellations which should enlighten the world for ages, you drag within the magic circle of your dullness, subjects not at all adapted to the purposes of the stage, and debase as he exalted. For instance, you take the uncompleted books of living authors, fresh from their hands, wet from the press, cut, hack, and carve them to the powers and capacities of your actors, and the capability of your theatres, finish unfinished works, hastily and crudely vamp up ideas not yet worked out by their original projector, but which have doubtless cost him many thoughtful days and sleepless nights; by a comparison of incidents and dialogue, down to the very last word he may have written a fortnight before, do your utmost to anticipate his plot — all this without his permission, and against his will; and then, to crown the whole proceeding, publish in some mean pamphlet, an unmeaning farrago of garbled extracts from his work, to which your name as author, with the honourable distinction annexed, of having perpetrated a hundred other outrages of the same description. Now, show me the distinction between such pilfering as this, and picking a man's pocket in the street:

"COME AND HAVE A GO IF YOU THINK
YOU'RE HARD ENOUGH!!!"

unless, indeed, it be, that the legislature has a regard for pocket-handkerchiefs, and leaves men's brains, except when they are knocked out by violence, to take care of themselves."

The hall erupted into uproar. Witty punters started throwing their snot-rags at the stage but few hit the mark. Chas moved to the side of the podium so he stood exposed, making "Come and Have a Go If You Think You're Hard Enough" gestures with both hands.

I was standing at the back and could make it out the open door behind me if it started to kick off and go pear-shaped. I pulled out my piece to be on the safe side. A strapping youth in a comically exaggerated tweed cap suddenly sprinted down the aisle and leapt on the stage squaring off against the plucky Limey scribe. Dickens was obviously not in tip-top condition but he didn't look too bothered. He had the benefit of experience, and being a Limey too. As the assailant moved in putting up his fists in a Marquis of Queensberry stance, Dickens quickly grabbed a handy pointer thing off the podium and started smacking him around the head with it. It made a fantastic swishing noise as it cleaved the air and a good thwack when it connected. Nice! The young guy covered his head with his hands and cowered, staggering backwards and tripping up. Then Chas put the boot in. After a couple of goes, the Yank was in a foetal stance pissing and shitting himself over the stage and everyone in the audience had forgotten their anger and was having a good throaty laugh at him. Well, not quite everyone. A couple of official looking dudes came up to Dickens, gently relieved him of the now broken pointer thingy, and led him quietly offstage like the towel-wallah routine that James Brown used to always do at his show. And just like the Godfather of Soul, Chas couldn't resist breaking free and returning for a couple of swift but meaty bonus kicks before going quietly. The hall exploded into cheers and applause and massed stamping of feet. I noticed a tasty bird in a crinoline skirt beside me.

"That was pretty fucked up!" I yelled over the hubbub, but she just ignored me. "I said, THAT WAS PRETTY FUCKED UP!" I said but she still ignored me. Then I heard this really really annoying high pitched noise getting louder and louder I I I felt I I was blacking out.

SONG OF A BAKER

The following day the professional jismologist was having a scone and a cup of tea in the park just like before. He hoped nothing interesting was going to happen today and he was right. A beggar came up.

"That looks like a nice scone," went The Beggar.

"I don't like scones much... but I fucking love butter and jam. You can have the scone if you like... I've licked it though."

The Beggar pretended not to hear. He still had a modicum of self-respect. "I used to love making scones. I used to be a baker in the olden days. I had a nice shop. My dad and his grandad had it before me and I grew up there playing with knives and dangerous machinery. Sharp things. Hot things. Poisonous things. You name it. When I inherited the bakery I had a girl who worked for me who'd often give me a blow-job in the kitchen. I had it made."

"How come you fucked up?" Not that he cared.

"One day a bloke came in and tried to steal a loaf. I nabbed him and he apologised and said he was so hungry he didn't know what he was doing. I told him it was wrong to steal off people and if he needed to eat he should thieve off the massive supermarket chain that had set up next door. He said he'd tried there first but they'd sold out of bread. I told him to fuck off and steal some flour and yeast from them and fucking bake himself a loaf. He said he didn't know how to bake bread so I copied out my granddad's recipe for him and told him to fuck off."

"That was nice of you. Did he?"

"Yes... He came in the next day and gave me massive cheese he'd pinched from next door to say thanks. Fucking massive Camembert...Delicious. I wish I still had it. "

"You can't have your cheese and eat it."

"You can't eat cheese you haven't got."

"Please go on. I'm on tenterhooks here."

"Well he got well into baking after that and started feeding all his poor mates and then flogging loaves to supplement his dole cheque. Eventually he could buy a car and he started delivering. You can see where this is going?"

"I'm afraid so."

"Eventually the cunt put me out of business and now he lives in a palace up to his neck in Russian hookers and cocaine from everywhere. There's no justice."

Our heroic albeit tedious bastard wasn't sure what to say to that so he just started laughing uproariously and jumped up and took to his heals.

1992

Negativland formed in the San Francisco Bay Area, nexus of the first Summer of Love, in the late seventies. Their experimental bent was overt from the outset by virtue of their taking the name of both their group and their label from songs by radical kosmische rockers Neu! in the first of their many appropriations. Since their eponymous debut in 1980, Negativland released a number of albums with tracks ranging from pure collage to more tuneful affairs. These completely uncommercial efforts were released on their own label until they signed to SST Records, home of us "punk" and "post-punk" acts such as Black Flag, The Minutemen, Firehose, Hüsker Dü, The Descendents and Bad Brains.

Their first release for SST, 1987's *Escape From Noise* gained them a wider audience, amplified by their media-baiting culture-jamming promotional techniques which were imaginative and sometimes ethically questioned. Following the somewhat unexpected relative success of this album, the group created a press release claiming a link between their song "Christianity is Stupid" and a quadruple familicide. The ensuing scandal from the media

stunt became the foundation for one side of Negativland's next release, *Helter Stupid*, which sampled news broadcasts of the coverage, more Rev. Estus Pirkle (from the same sermon used on "Christianity is Stupid"), an interview with Charles Manson, and what was the band's most brazenly unauthorised sample to date, The Beatles' "Helter Skelter" obviously. In 1992 the group followed up with an overtly humorous tribute record entitled *U2* that initiated a lawsuit with U2's record label and then subsequently their own label. This case took a terrible personal toll and almost destroyed Negativland as a band, but reciprocally it increased their market profile dramatically and they were able to capitalise on their practical experience of copyright and bring the associated issues to the status of legitimacy as a subject matter in popular music. The group continued to address other social issues too, and the follow-up to *U2*, entitled *Guns*, focussed on gun control and included samples familiar from Steinski's masterwork cited earlier.

A dosser came up to me. He was dressed in a suit and making an effort at least.

"Some cunt just gave me this."

He handed me a pound coin… except I quickly noticed it two five-pence pieces that had been super-glued together and spray-painted gold.

"Look at it!"

I did.

"It's not even worth five pence! I'd have to take it home and chisel it apart and soak the coins in paint-stripper and then it would only be ten pence. It's hardly worth it. Fuck. Even if I got a few of em and did em at the same time. Bollocks!"

"Cheeky bastard." I handed it back. "It'll still work in a vending machine though. Get some fags or something…"

"Oh yeah. Cheers. I hadn't thought of that."

"Just don't put it a fucking fruit machine. They always know the difference."

"You're a fucking expert."

"Yes. It's true. Here's a real pound so you can tell as well. Hang on to it for future reference or fucking gamble it. I don't give a fuck. It's just a pound."

"It might be just a pound for you mate but yeah it's a pound. Yeah."

Then he went. He might have fucking thanked me. It was a fucking pound after all.

22 November 1994 was a black day for bootleggers, not because it was the 31st anniversary of the JFK assassination but because it was the day when The Artist Then Was Then Known As Prince's sixteenth studio LP received it's first official albeit limited public release.

The album had originally been planned for release on 7 December 1987. It was referred to as "█" or "The Black Album" due to the album's monochromatic cover design bearing no title and not even the artist's name. The LP was seen by some as Prince's attempt to win back credibility among his fans who might have been African-Americans.

Characteristically, just before the album was released to the market Prince abandoned the entire project and recalled all copies leaving only around a hundred promotional copies in circulation.

A number of theories have been postulated for the album's suppression: (A) Prince had become convinced that the album was intrinsically evil or at best represented an ominous portent; (B) he experienced a crisis of conscience over the eroticism and violence of its lyrics; (C) he decided to scrap the album after a bad ecstasy trip.

Either way, immediately following the deletion counterfeit and bootleg copies of the release emerged. David Altschul, General Counsel at Warner Brothers Records Inc. at the

#	Album	Artist	Year
1	**Self-titled** (brown)	The Band	**1969**
2	**Self-titled** (black)	The Damned	**1980**
3	**Self-titled** (black)	Metallica	**1991**
4	**Untitled** (black)	Prince	**1987**
5	**The Brown Album**	The Child Molesters	**1994**
6	**Self-titled** (grey)	Echo and the Bunnymen	**1994**
7	**The Yellow Album**	The Simpsons	**1998**
8	**The Black Album**	Jay-Z	**2003**
9	**The Grey Album**	Danger Mouse	**2004**
10	**The White Albun**	Tism	**2004**

time claimed that it was "probably the most bootlegged album in history!"

To clarify the nomenclature of illicit recordings: a "counterfeit" is an unauthorised issue of an existing recording intended to resemble the appearance of the original as closely as possible in an attempt to deceive the buyer; a "pirate" is an unauthorised copy that does not pretend to be otherwise; and a "bootleg" makes available recordings that are otherwise unavailable. Each variant provides different ethical conundrums and record dealers have individually divergent attitudes to each type of release.

Prince's album was issued by many sources in different unofficial editions and the status of each issue would change contingent on the status of the official release.

Notwithstanding its illegality, several celebrities, including U2's frontmen The Edge and Bono, cited it as one of their favourite albums of the year in *Rolling Stone* magazine's celebrity poll. I expect Negativland saw the funny side. Seven years later, on the week of the album's official (albeit limited edition) release the record company ran an ad in *Billboard* offering owners of bootleg copies a free copy of the legitimate release in exchange. This was viewed by many as an entrapment ploy. The official release was then deleted on 27 January 1995.

Prince's record was one of many to exploit the Beatles' idea of monochromatic eponymous records. The Fab Four had themselves issued matching compilations in 1973 that were often referred to as "The Red Album" and "The Blue Album" respectively. The trope went on to become especially popular with comedians, novelty acts and cartoon characters—The Beatles having had their own cartoon series running from 1965 to 1969 of course.

After he'd got a couple of blocks from the unfortunate baker, the knackered old writer stopped momentarily and looked at his watch. This didn't make any sense. He didn't have anywhere to go and no-one was expecting him anywhere as far as he knew so it must have been just a reflex. Like I said his watch was a cheap Taiwan digital LCD job. He'd found in a park and it still ran okay but some of the segments had gone wonky and sometimes it was easy to read and sometimes impossible depending on the time.

Seven segment representations of numerals appeared in US patents in the early twentieth century as a technique for transmitting numbers telegraphically but they didn't become popular until the advent of LED technology in the 1970s.

Each of the ten numerals of the decimal system can be abstracted into a pattern of seven lines. This potentially gives us 128 possible states, eleven of which are used for decimal notation. The shape of any of these numerals is of course dependent on the binary configuration of respective input voltages. The segments are traditionally signified A-G clockwise with the top bar being A and the crossbar being G. The underlying shape of the segments is therefore the same as a figure

	ABCDEFG binary	decimal	no. segments
(blank)	0000000	0	0
0	1111110	126	6
1	0110000	48	2
2	1101101	109	5
3	1111001	121	5
4	0110011	51	4
5	1011011	91	5
6	1011111	95	6
7	1110000	112	3
8	1111111	127	7
9	1111011	123	6

"8" but is better understood poetically as an infinity symbol rotated through one dimension.

Although the numeric representations seem uncontroversial to us now, in the 1970s the abstractions (especially for numbers 4 and 7) appeared so contrived as to be mnemonic rather than representational. The symbols looked like gibberish at first but people soon got used to them; although it was particularly harsh on innumerate people who could otherwise have benefitted the most from the new electronic calculators.

Of course, anyone completely unfamiliar with Arabic numerals would have trouble understanding what was going on at all. The number of segments illuminated for a digit was completely unrelated to the quantity being described. If one were trying to intuitively reconstruct the sequence it may not even be obvious that we are dealing with a numeric base of ten, since "space"—the blank cell with no segments lit—is not equivalent to zero in our system of representation.

An interesting anomaly arises here, the first three nonzero digits (1, 2, 3) are smaller quantities than the number of segments needed to represent them. The next three (4, 5, 6) equal the number of segments needed to represent them, and the last three (7, 8, 9) exceed the number of segments needed to represent them. This conforms to the law of inverse relations.

In the analysis of any unknown form, the search for symmetry is a useful starting point. We find that "2" and "5" possess reflectional symmetry, whilst "6" and "9" possess rotational symmetry. "0" and "8" possess both, whilst "3", "4" and "7" are completely asymmetrical. It seems likely that these latter figures would be classified provisionally as a different class of symbols distinct from the symmetric examples. "1" is deeply problematic and space precludes discussion here.

It might be amusing to imagine the segments as a species of cellular automata along the lines of John Conway's *Game of Life* and to try to determine the evolutionary rules that govern the evolution of the digits in sequence.

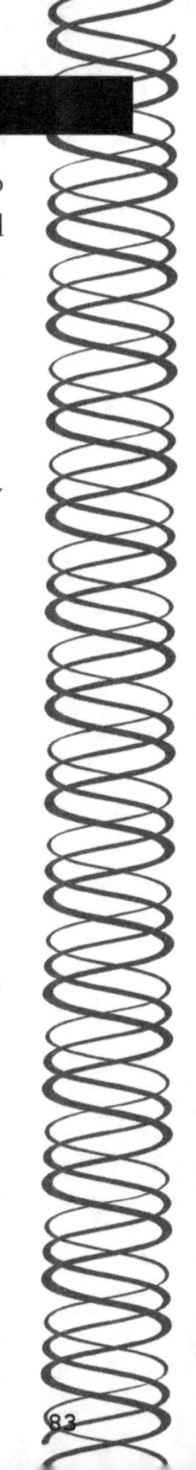

The Bastardizer came to and he was strapped into what seemed to be the same swively chair that he had fucked off in all those years ago.

"X-Rays."

"Pulse?"

"Pulse normal."

"Breathing steady."

"Electrolytic cream." She started smearing crazy jelly crap on random bits of me. That was good.

"Clamp."

"It looks fine."

"Small probe."

"Pulse 85 increasing."

"Relax!"

"Cream, nurse."

"Right."

"Switch on the cerebral pulsator."

"Give me the electrodes."

"She is introducing the electrodes into the frontal area."

"This is the critical part."

"Pulse?"

"Steady at 89."

"Good. Electrodes in position. I'll take over. She's about to apply the current. One mistake now and…"

"Oh fuck! Not again!"The Bastardizer inadvertently spewed down his shirt-front. It was the first time in the whole book that he'd been glad he hadn't had that bacon sandwich that I mentioned earlier.

"That'll go nicely with the stain on your strides," went The Stripper. She was leaning over him with a clipboard, her eyes glassy behind her glasses and quite good cleavage-scoping potential.

"Uh?" Went the timesick Bastardizer, noticed the wetness in his kecks where he'd pissed himself without realising. "Oh. Fucking hell. Is that it? A machine that makes you piss yourself? What's wrong with beer?"

"You don't get Charles Dickens with beer," she went.

"You do in my fucking local!" Went The Bastardizer. He thought she'd said "Chicken-in-a-Basket". That was another weird side-effect.

"You returned to our time zone a couple of moments before you left. That's why you heard the pre-launch check twice."

"Oh yeah. Where's my chicken?"

"The Chron-O-Funnel™ is a uniplex device so you can only go backwards in time."

"I see. That doesn't explain where my chicken is though. But surely the temporal paradoxes that would be produced would be more catastrophic going backwards than forwards? Since we wouldn't know the consequences of those are."

"No paradoxes are possible since you're intangible to the customers in the past time-frames."

"Yeah you say that but what if I acted on the knowledge I derived and thereby changed the future?
Wouldn't punters using this machine subsequent to
my trip see divergences between their history and the
one they went back to?"

The Stripper chuckled heartily, "People don't act
on knowledge derived from excursions into the past.
It's a phenomena that's never been observed. Actually,
people don't act on knowledge at all. Ever!" Actually
she said "full stop" but I'm still a bit pissed right now
and I couldn't figure out how to write that.

"Hmmmmmmmmmmmmmm..." went The Bastardizer, "mmmmmmm-mm-mmm-mmm"

"Sorry, my finger slipped."

"That's a shame. There's a small part of me that
would like to know what the future is like. Maybe
other people feel the same way."

"It's called curiosity."

The Stripper flipped a switch on the console and
the straps binding his ankles and wrists made a spro-
inging noise, but didn't open. She had to come over
and pry them apart with a screwdriver. At one point,
the tool slipped and gouged him in the wrist.

"Shit!" Went the Bastardizer, "That hurts!"

The Stripper helped him out of the chair and supported his groggy frame as they lumbered intermina-
bly slowly back to main room.

"This is a CGI simulation of life in the year 2020," she
went. "Thirty-three years from now."

IT WAS AN IMPRESSIVE VOLUME BUT TO
TELL THE TRUTH I WAS A BIT REPULSED

The Stripper went over and fiddled with the VCR The Bastardizer was reassured to see a technology that he was familiar with despite his disgust at the ingenious contraption that had only a few non-copyright-violating applications. A picture came on the screen.

The screen showed a clinical white room which looked a lot like the lab next door. There were a dozen fat blokes sat along one wall, naked except for big nappies with hoses coming out of them connected to a sewer. They all had big folds of blubbery fat and if you looked close you could see clear tubes that had been plugged in subcutaneous. Coloured liquids pulsed up and down them. The Bastardizer found himself thinking of walruses. The blokes all looked comatose but occasionally one of them would fart, belch or sneeze with comic exaggeration. All of them were wearing these massive sixties style goggles.

It wasn't very interesting. Then I suddenly noticed one of the blokes fiddling with his nappy. There was a big bulge in his groinic area. He freed his prick, which could have been medium or average in size but you couldn't accurately get it to scale. It was semi-hard and it suddenly sprayed a huge gout of greenish jissom into the air. It was an impressive volume but to tell the truth I was a bit repulsed.

"Uh. What's with the goggles? Is the spunk radioactive?"

"They're holographic projection glasses. They're getting the latest and best in immersive hardcore pornography."

"They're a bunch of bloody specs maniacs if you ask me. Is this customary? How long do they spend like that?"

"All the time. Pretty much everyone. That's it. That's what people do in the future. All of it."

"Why are they only blokes? What about the ladies?"

"They need different equipment so there's a separate lab, or bedroom. We prefer the traditional terminology"

"How do you keep up with demand? I assume they're not watching footage of themselves sitting there spouting. No-one could get off on that."

"The cyberfilth is generated by a global network of computers all interconnected. Like they would have to be for it to be a network. They have been programmed to generate Infinite PrOn using techniques derived from chaos physics. They have all the characters and potential positions and they permute them inna fractal stylee."

"Don't the punters get fed up of it?"

"All kinds of media are available. They can switch from immersive visual to normal 2D films, or to sex-audio or literary erotica. No-one ever gets fed up with it. Ever!

"Lots of hardcore porn films will include a reference to a magazine or book as an acknowledgement of the intrinsic power of a word-dimension, or the *w*-axis as we call it, and also use music as expansion of the sound-dimension, or *s*-axis, though grunts, shouts and squelching noises are usually more important from a stimulatory viewpoint. These synchronise the *s* and *w* axes as specifically as the *i*-axis is fixed by the images. This is why undubbed (and unsubtitled) foreign language porno films are no less effective from a physiological perspective.

"Some species, most notably frogs, have a language entirely devoted to sex. This used to be regarded as a primitive stage, but now we see it as the ultimate stage of the evolution of a language. The origins of computer generated pornography can be traced to a research programme funded by this very organisation in about four years time."

"Well. I dunno if it looks so bad after all."

"But just imagine. With the content being endlessly permuted, we can't possibly copyright all the output. Only the programs themselves and the source material. Gillions of bytes of output and no royalties at all for the omninational corporations that dominate the combinatorial porno industry. It breaks my heart! "

"Well. That's me convinced. So… If this is the future, can it be stopped?"

"No. We don't think it can. But we have decided that you should go back in time and kill the cunt who thought it all up just on the off chance that it works."

"Woah! Back up there! How do you mean 'we have decided that you should go back in time and kill the cunt who thought it all up just on the off chance that it works.' We who? Me why? Kill what! Cunt who? Where? Eh? When?"

"Let me put it all on the table," she continued. "That's better… I have been sent back from the future where I was involved with the project that gave rise to the first and greatest work of CGP, albeit obliquely. Albeit obliquely," she said it twice because she liked the sound of it so much. "I have to persuade you to perform a special mission. An… assassination if you like. Since this future is sort of our fault and we have the time machines to do it now anyway."

"Who did you choose me?"

She laughed for a long time, "because you're THE BASTARDIZER!" She went. She was right about that.

"Okay," I went, "If you're from the future, how come you're not all intangible like I was? And if we're about to fuck off all those temporal paradoxes with some hilarious gag, can I have a go on some of those goggles please?"

"Fucking what?!" She went, "oh, alright. Don't hold your breath. Cunt."

▶ *A* **A** *A* **A** *A* **A** *U* ▶ **U** *B*

▶ **U** *B* ▶ **A** *A* **I** **O** **U** **I** **O** **U**

E **I** **O** **U** *E* **I** **O** *B* **E** **I** **O** **U** ▶

O **D** *Q* **D** ▶ **D** *N* **Q** *O* **I** *E*

Q **W** **U** **I** *O* **U** **B** **I** **Q** **X** *U*

I **Q** *U* ▶ **I** **Q** *U* **Q** **I** ▶ **U**

Q **I** ▶ *U* **W** *J* **X** *U* **W** **X**

W **E** **J** *C* **J** *U* ▶ **I** *O* **I** **O** **X**

I *O* **I** **O** **X** *B* **I** **O** **X** **I** *O* **I** **O** **X**

U *U* **I** **U** *E* **D** **I** **U** *E* **D** **J** **U**

J *C* **E** **C** **J** **U** *U* **D** **D** *E* **J**

"I can't say it did much for me. Does that mean I'm gay?"

"I doubt it. Do you remember the first time you saw porn? Could you fully process what you were seeing?"

"I'm not an expert. That would have been about five years ago when one my mates got a tape of Gerard Damiano's *Deep Throat* off some bikers he knew. It was a tenth gen dub and we huddled around the telly watching the colours bleed psychedelically. We thought they'd duped him with some weird experimental film instead of a porno. You couldn't tell what you were watching at all. We all got pissed and had a laugh about it. Nobody wanked as far as I know. The toilet was just off the lounge so it would been obvious if anyone had tried to bang off a crafty one. Mind you…" I reflected… "I do recall that night I had the most intense erotic dream of my entire life. Something about a nude blonde French bird on a train. We were going like the clappers. When I woke up I had to chip myself out of bed with a toffee hammer…"

"Quite so… The effect of course is very different depending on whether you've ever actually had sex or not."

"Are these blokes virgins then?"

"Yes. Technically. In the future actual sex is done with test tubes."

"And they say there's no such thing as progress!"

The experimental knucklehead was ambling along in the afternoon sunshine fiddling with a hole in his trouser pocket and enjoying the tactile experience. He was chuffed as fuck to discover a fifty pence piece skulking in the lining and so he headed for the bus station where there was a dilapidated ex-ambulance that would do a cup of tea and a slice of bread and lard pudding: a terrible greasy grey slab impregnated with carbonised sultanas like the ball bearings that the anarchists liked to put in their infernal devices in the olden days.

Whilst he was blowing the steam off the top of the black liquid in the hollow truncated conical section of expanded polystyrene, or cup if you prefer, he watched the buses come and go, moving petulant families and lonely individuals, unified only by their shared thriftiness, enforced or otherwise, from one place to another like some kind of shit-shovelling machine that had been cunningly modified to accept human beings.

"Here he is…" went the stout fellow behind the counter. It seemed portentous he said this coz he'd not even said hello when the writer bought his scoff.

The old experimental filth-maker watched with growing disconcert as a character came up to him, notable for wearing a battered top hat on top of his general shabbiness. The hat was battered as in tatty not as in dipped in a mixture of flour, milk and egg and then deep-fried. In this respect it differed from most of the other phenomena that had manifested in the proximity of the mobile cafe.

"Have you got a moment?" Went The Character.

"So long as you don't want it rendered into legal tender."

"What?"

"I haven't got any money."

"Do you want to see a trick?"

"I'm looking at one," went our protagonist pretending to mishear a us pejorative for the male genitalia in the feeble hope that gratuitous though tiny rudeness would deter the beggar.

The Character produced a deck of cards from his pocket, "Take one of these."

The old writer didn't want to get involved but The Character had just somehow magically transformed himself into a kind of conjurer and he invoked an automatic reflex.

"♠7"

"Don't tell me!" Went The Prestidigitator, snatching back the card and offering the pack again so this time the old writer took one.

"♥Q"

"GAH!!!" The annoyed Thaumaturgist was visibly pissed off now, he held the pack at arms length and drew a card himself at random, and handed it to the writer facing away from him. "Now…"

"♦ J"

"Fuck off ! How can I do the trick if you keep doing that?!"

"Well, obviously, If I just tell you what the card is then you don't need to go to all the bother of doing the whole elaborate trick. It seems more efficient. You can save your magic up and conjure up a nice house to live in."

Then the old bastard pulled a packet of fags out of his pocket and proffered them. The Conjurer forgot his petulance and took one.

"And your cigarette is a Players Navy Cut I believe," went the old writer, touching his fingertips to his temples as if he was a mentalist and generously subtracting another fifteen minutes of misery from The Conjurer's estimated life-span.

His new pal shook his hand and did that thing where you reach round and pat the other's back. The old writer never cared much for that but didn't suspect, like you obviously would, that he'd planted something on him. As he left, the writer noticed a playing card was stuck in the ribbon of The Conjurer's hat. It was the seven of spades. The Lord of Unstable effort. Labour in Vain. Off in the distance there was the sound of a huge explosion. And a sinister mushroom cloud appeared over the rooftops.

"Was that a fuckin bomb?"

"Couldn't be. There's no such thing as bombs."

"How come?"

"Well, if a bomb doesn't explode, it's a dud not a bomb, and if it does explode then it destroys itself in the explosion so it doesn't exist then either. And you can't know if a potential bomb is a dud or not without seeing if it explodes. It's like Shrödinger's Cat with a bomb instead of a cat."

24:02:2004

On 14 November 2003, Shawn Corey Carter (aka Jay-Z) released his own record called *The Black Album*, his eighth studio album. It debuted at number one on the US *Billboard* charts, sold almost half-a-million copies in its first week, was acclaimed by critics and nominated for a Grammy Award. In line with then-current marketing trends his label released an acapella version of the album to encourage unofficial re-mixes. In February the following year, NYC-born UK-resident DJ Danger Mouse combined these vocal tracks with samples exclusively from the Beatles' *White Album* to create *The Grey Album*. The project was originally created just for his friends but was soon hailed as the maddest mash-up project ever and quickly spread over THE INTERNET. Danger Mouse hadn't sought permis-sion from any of the copyright owners of the underlying works to use their music. Jay-Z and his label had released the acap-pella version so that others could sample his music and did not pursue any action against Danger Mouse. However, despite

the fact that both Jay-Z and Paul McCartney expressed their approval of the project, the owner of the Beatles' sound recording copyrights and the owner of the compositions on *The White Album* sent Danger Mouse cease and desist letters and he immediately complied with their requests.

The general public's response wasn't quite as obedient and a day of coordinated electronic civil disobedience was called for 24 February 2004. Led by Downhill Battle, an activist group seeking to restructure the music industry. Participating websites posted copies of *The Grey Album* for free download on its sites for 24 hours in protest of the attempts to suppress the work. This protest was provoked by the opinion that the sampling is fair use and that a statutory license should be provided in the same manner as if a song had been covered. Hundreds of web sites participated and roughly 170 hosted the album for download. Over 100,000 copies were downloaded on that day alone. The legal repercussions of the protest were minimal; a number of the participants received cease and desist letters from EMI, but no charges were filed in connection with the event.

The Grey Album soon became super popular with both the general audience and critics, with *Rolling Stone* calling it the ultimate remix record and *Entertainment Weekly* later ranking it the best record of that year.

As observed earlier, in the depths of his psychosis Charles Manson had mashed up the Beatles' recordings with his idiosyncratic reading of The Book of Revelation in a drug-addled attempt at a blueprint for race war and it had catastrophic PR results for the hippie movement all over the world except for the USSR. It's just as well Manson hadn't heard of Demis Rous-sos's outfit, Aphrodite's Child, and their epic 1972 double-LP *666* or who knows what would have happened.

But we digress, with *The Grey Album* Danger Mouse was able to wield his mad skillz to successfully produce a miscegi-nated synthesis of the traditional white musical icons with the contemporary black musical icon, reconciling the black and white, the ancient and modern, the critical and commercial, the amplic and decadent. Who is the third who walks always beside you? Eh?

NOT MANY HAPPY RETURNS

It had been a reasonably jam-packed day for me and it was only early evening but I had to head home to get loaded and watch telly. Also, I wanted to have a go in the limo I'd been assigned. Having sampled the mini-bar, I was drowsy and dozed as my driver made slow progress through the arse-end of the peak-hour traffic. We pulled up at the pelican outside the old orphanage. The kids seemed to be having fun. There were party sounds of children laughing and shouting coming out and sporadic gunfire… or more likely bursting balloons.

An endless procession of elderly twats and young taxpayer couples pushing cheap baby-strollers saun-tered lazily across the zebra crossing in front of us. It was not without relief that I noted the green pedestri-an signal start to flash. But then some tiny old bastard with a Zimmer frame started to cross, directly disregarding the directives of the signal. His ancient form was twisted in painful spasm and there was no way he was going to make it across in time. As he came directly in front of the limousine he paused to manoeuvre round an artfully placed dog turd. At least I hoped it was a dog turd. This old twat was an unparalleled expert when it came to tardiness, with decades of dawdling behind him, and he knew exactly what he was taking ages to do. He stared straight through the windscreen at us with an accusing expression but I was completely vague what he was accusing us of. I cursed the vagaries of justice that currently prevented me from having any jurisdiction in the field of traffic legislation. I would have liked to shoot him you see.

"This is reminding me of times in the past when I felt very annoyed…" observed the driver.

The old fucker finally made the safety of the kerb and I was relieved to see that I wasn't as old and feeble as he was by then. We pulled away from the lights smooth and easy in the overpriced status symbol we were driving in.

Suddenly I realised something! I had been so transfixed by this hideous but out-of-brief procrastinative spectacle that I had overlooked the ambient sound from the orphanage opposite. It was a birthday party and I had a hunch! Not on my back like the one that tardy bastard just had either! The other kind.

"Stäedler!" I yelled, since that was the chauffeur's name, "Pull over!"

Stäedler rolled his eyes and sharply applied the brake. I smacked my teeth into the back of his head-rest by accident.

"Duuuurrrshh! Wrrreeeennnjj…" I instructed him, clutching my hurt gob with one had and opening the door with the other I leapt out the side and wiped out a lycra-clad wanker in the bike-lane. He went psychopath on the cyclepath.

"Why don't you look where you're going!?" He raged indignantly.

"Ith nob ath thumby!!" I raged back, expectorating flecks of blood at him, whilst whipping out my piece and smacking him across the side of the noggin with it. He instantly regretted investing in a stupid and expensive streamlined helmet that only protected the top of his head.

Then I made my way round the back of the orphanage to crouch outside the window for the lights to go out and the inevitable moment. It made my blood boil. The single most blatant and regular instance of copyright violation in history ever. An epidemic that had started in the US, spread to Europe, heedless of language barriers, and now virulently contaminated all continents, including the research bases in the Polar Regions where the highly-qualified scientists should have known better. Not in Africa quite so much though.

I refer of course to "Happy Birthday". The most covered song of all time that had been published by schoolteachers Mildred and Patty Hill in 1893 as "Good Morning to All" in their book *Song Stories for the Kindergarten*. The combination of melody and lyrics in "Happy Birthday to You" first appeared in print in 1912 and probably existed even earlier. None of these early appearances included credits or copyright notices. The Summy Company registered for copyright in 1935 crediting authors Preston Ware Orem and Mrs. R.R. Forman. In 1988, Warner/Chappell purchased the company owning the copyright for $25 million, with the value of "Happy Birthday" estimated at $5 million. Based on the 1935 copyright registration, Warner claims that the United States copyright will not expire until 2030 and that unauthorised public performances of the song remain illegal unless royalties are paid to Warner.

I simply could not fathom the psychology of a person who would choose to make the theft of imaginary property the central feature of a children's birthday celebration. The fact that these scum implicated their children in their crimes made me wretch. And indeed I did at that point choose to make physical my disgust. I must have overdone it at the limo mini-bar.

The hubbub inside began to die down and the lights went out. This was it! The kids struck up the familiar words and I edged away from the window intending to kick in the back door. It was just as well I did, as at that moment the entire window blew outwards, shattering itself and was followed by a huge ball of flame.

"WHOOMPH!" Said the fireball, only much louder and more impressive. The carnage was pretty much along the lines of what you would expect.

I assumed that the person carrying the cake, lighted candles and all, had stumbled in the darkened room and ignited something highly flammable. It was a scenario more common than one would imagine. In fact I was sick of reading about it happening, not because I felt sorry for the would-be criminals but because it was getting boring.

Fortunately I wasn't all singed, having been sheltered by my position in the doorway. I decided the most useful thing I could do to help would be to get back to the limo and get it out the way so the fire brigade could come and clean up.

As Stäedler drove me home I speculated on the ambiguous nature of the explosion. Not only had a criminal offence had been prevented in itself, but the offenders were now prevented from their inevitable descent into ever-escalating criminality. Given that irony was the organising principle of The Universe it seemed likely that some of the incinerated children would have gone on to become arsonists or pyromaniacs or perhaps both. You can't cheat karma.

They year had started with George W. Bush being sworn in as US President for a second term. Now better remembered for his linguistic innovations than for his statesmanship, or lack thereof, he is simultaneously one of the most and least popular US presidents in history; receiving record-breaking ratings in the wake of the 2001 aircraft attacks but one of the lowest ratings during the financial crisis that marked his second term.

It's hard to convey how scary things had got in the early-noughties following the War on Terror and then the War on Everything Else. Even the spectacularly inoffensive Dixie Chicks got sent to a gulag for speaking their brains and nobody wanted to be the next them.

A ray of musical hope was provided unexpectedly when Green Day, a widely derided but wildly popular pop-punk trio from Berkeley, CA, put out *American Idiot* in September 2004. It was a State of the Union address-styled concept punk-rock-opera full of power chords and slogans with an odd Oi! tinge to it. The melodies were so familiar that it was almost inevitable that someone would do a mash-up to out the punksters on any potential "subconscious plagiarism" that might be going on. So mash-up artists Kode 9 and Party Ben did that exactly and then some more. Released on 18 November under the moniker Dean Gray, their disc kicked Green Day's original out of the park. Using *American Idiot* as a starting point, they grafted on samples of Oasis's "Wonderwall", various U2 tunes, Lalo Schifrin's "Theme from *Mission: Impossible*", Buffalo Springfield's "For What It's Worth" ("Fortunate Son" by Creedence being a near the bone for Dubya we expect) plus The Beatles' "A Day in the Life" and, inevitably, "Blackbird". The musical potpourri was complimented with imaginative speechifying from luminaries such as JFK and Bill Hicks.

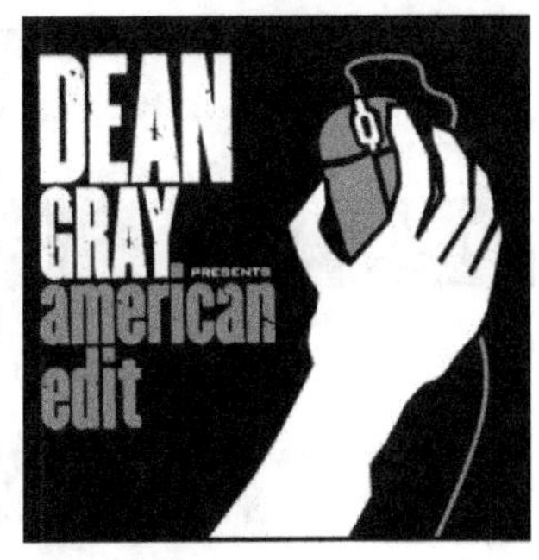

Usefully, on 26 March 2005 *Dr Who* had finally returned to screens full of thinly veiled allegories of Cruel Britannia starring Christopher Eccleston as Nine.

The show had been AWOL for fifteen years or so having been canned on 6 December 1989 a year or so after the KLF's number one smash hit with a mash-up of the theme tune. The KLF's cut was in turn liberally sampled on the *American Edit* standout track "Dr Who on Holiday", a recursive mash-up of The Timelords' original mash-up that postulates occult links between The Bush Jr. Administration (quoting his speech at Fort Hood, TX, on 3 January 2003) and the actual fucking Daleks themselves (from episode six of "Genesis of the Daleks" originally broadcast 12 April 1975).

The name "Dean Gray" was of course a spoonerism of "Green Day" and a reference to Grey Tuesday. But if the surname had been anglicised to "Dean Grey" it would have been an true anagram of "Green Day" as well as matching the spelling on Danger Mouse's record that they were named in honour of. Why would you do that? It doesn't matter, as I write this texts, films and musics now have almost perfect mobility in time and space due to THE INTERNET. You get pretty much anything from anytime right now. It didn't use to be like that. The next thing you know it will be things. And then people… Progress is necessary. Plagiarism implies it.

IT IS ALWAYS 1987

The basement of the library was where they kept all the old shit that no-one ever took out and this was where the old bastard liked to come for a furtive wank every so often. He'd never seen another soul down here, or body for that matter. There was a rack way up the back that everyone had forgot but it was full with bound copies of crazy good pickings from prerevolutionary times.

He thought that he'd start today with an old chestnut and made his way direct to the shelf on autopilot and reached up with two hands to take down the massive leather volume. Bigger than a phone book, it was identical to twelve other volumes on the shelf with not even a blind stamp to distinguish it. Some of the volumes had little typed labels at the base of the spine but this one, and some others, just had a little square of dried adhesive where the label had peeled off decades back.

The old writer lugged the volume back to a carrel and sat down and made himself comfy. He was leafing through the tome looking for the filthy pictures and starting to.

"That creepy old creep comes in almost every day," went the miserable little cleaner to the Foxy

Librarian, attempting pathetically to ingratiate himself. "He gives me the creeps."

"He seems harmless enough," went the contrarian librarian. She had a heavy Eastern European accent that I won't bother to try here. She was a Hungarian Librarian too.

"He just uses the khazi and reads the papers. And I've seen him helping himself to cups of tea in the staff corner. There's a sign says quite clearly that's for staff use only."

"It's doesn't really matter. The warning sign limits the abuse to a manageable level. If it was a significant problem we'd lock it up, but then we'd have to issue keys to all the staff and it would cost more to police than we lost."

"But it's the principle! Free tea and coffee is a perk for the staff, not the public."

"Well, first, he's not the public, he's a customer. And second, you're not staff either, you're a contractor. So if it comes to that you're ten times worse than him on the grounds that it's you that feels that way. He might stink of piss but at least he doesn't stink of hypocrisy."

"I should report you!"

"Is it paradoxical that sewage workers are well versed in personal hygiene? I don't think so. I think it's actually the opposite. You know, if you weren't a twat, and you weren't so ugly and unpleasant, you might have stood a chance of a quick wrist job. But as it stands, I tire of you…"

At that moment the old bastard came over with an enquiry. "Volume Seven appears to be missing," he went.

STACKS OF DOOM

The library was fuckin massive but it didn't seem to have many books in it. I went past rows of video-cassettes, then LPs and cassettes, spools of microfilm, fiches and weird media I didn't even recognise. Then I had a brainwave.

The basement of the library was where they kept all the books that never got checked out. I knew the cunt would be down here from his borrowing records. I was just screwing the silencer on my piece when the lift I was in hit the bottom with a jaunty bounce and I accidentally discharged a round into the floor. The stench of cordite enveloped through the car just as the doors jerked open. A tiny cleaning twat stood there with a mop and bucket.

"That wasn't me…" I went, pulling out my piece and levelling it in his mug "it was this!"

The cleaner fainted dead away into a puddle of piss that hadn't been there just before. Given that he'd be the one to have to clean it up, it seemed like it was his prerogative. As I exited the lift I clocked The Target at the enquiry desk talking to the Foxy Librarian. I could tell she was the Librarian because she had a cute bun. I could see that line coming back to haunt me if I ever got out on a spoken word tour. I shoved the gun back in my pocket and went over, casual like, to hear what he was saying but as I got there he finished and got up to go. I took the seat and watched him disappear between the racks and compactuses. He couldn't get out that way. The only exit was the lift that I could see from here or the fire-door to the staircase beside it, and that was alarmed.

"I think I know your friend." I went to the Librarian.

"Aren't you meant to have a password or something?"

"I can't be arsed with all that shit for kids. I got things to see and people to do. Was that him?"

"Who?"

"Him."

"Was he him? Yes," she went, unhelpfully.

"Oh fuck it. I'll kill him anyway." I got up and followed the bastard, cornering him by 741:548F.

"Oi!" I went, eloquent.

"Shhh!" She went, "Keep your fucking voice down. This is a library in case you hadn't noticed."

"This is a fucking 9mm Glock in case you hadn't noticed, you tedious pedant!" I pulled the piece out of my pocket or would have but it got snagged on a little hole it had made and discharged accidentally again. Actually I had no idea what a 9mm Glock was but I'd heard that in a film in a similar context.

"Fuck! Sorry!" I went. It had blown a blackened hole in the floor beside me. It made a noise like a cork going off when it discharged and another one like someone dropping a bowling ball on a watermelon when the shot hit the ground. The two sounds merged for everyone except a blind twat on the other side of the floor who looked round to see what had happened. I eventually unsnagged my weapon and drew a bead on the old writer. He stood there like a rabbit in the headlights, but only in as much as the expression on his face, and even that wasn't very much like a rabbit's admittedly. The Foxy Librarian was edging her way to the fire exit. That was understandable.

HOW THE MUSIC BUSINESS WORKS

"Empty your pockets." I instructed the old bastard helpfully.

"I haven't got any weapons," he went.

"Would you tell me if you did?"

"On the contrary, wouldn't I be likely to show you?"

"Look, it's grandad's operation procedure or whatever... okay? Empty them!" I cocked my weapon. Or at least I meant to but instead I accidentally let off another round that went into the shelf just behind his noggin. It took out some antique tome in an eruption of leather and paper.

"At least it wasn't a new one!" I went humorously.

"You could have had my fucking eye out with that! Fucking maniac!" The Target thought I'd done it on purpose and so he started to comply. As I'd expected, his pocket weren't at all interesting: Three swiss army knives; foreign currency; a pocket magnifying glass; small mirror; set of skeleton keys; a compass; a tea-bag; blood donor card.

I was distracted checking through his possessions so I didn't clock him reaching down the back of his pants in time to react. For an instant, I thought he was gonna pull out a concealed piece but instead he just produced a handful of steaming turd. It was a norrible ochre colour and well sloppy. Some drops and chunks fell through his fingers as he held it out to me.

"There's this too!" He went, and for a fraction of a second he regarded it then flung dung spinning at me.

"Shit!" Went I. "That's disgusting."

"Yeah," went the old writer, with an air of worldly resignation, "I know it is..."

It occurred to me that turds were technically copy-rightable works, in that each one was an original work with fixed properties. Presumably they would be covered under the same provisions as more formal-ly acknowledged sculpture. Indeed it was a strange chronological anomaly that permitted this rudimen-tary though profound insight before the shit hit me in the face, blinding me. I clawed at my eyes with my free hand and blundered hurtfully into a shelf. I was stunned. Lots of people had thrown shit at me over the years but no-one had ever connected before.

"GAH!" I went. Through my beshitted vision I expected to see the old bastard scarpering or even pouncing upon me in a moment but he was just standing there. Even though he had transferred ownership of the turd the residual intellectual property rights remained his.

"Have you got anything else in there?" I didn't feel like I had to be unpleasant since any moment I WAS GOING TO SHOOT THE CUNT IN THE HEAD ANYWAY.

"Only scorn and derision now. And there's too much of that for even The Bastardizer to make off with."

"Okay pal, enough with the chit-chat. I'm going to shoot you in the fucking head now. Any last words?"

The doomed fucker brandished a dusty volume at me and started holding forth.

"I've seen things you wouldn't believe... Some of them I still don't believe myself and I was the one who saw them in the first place. There were spectacular things to do with cosmic shit and stuff. Galaxies. The Milky Way. Mars Bars. I've lost my thread... Impressive things that blew me away at the time. And things that I only noticed years later. Maybe my things aren't that good measured by other people's experiences but they impressed me... at the time anyway. I wish I could think of some examples now. The circumstances at the moment aren't exactly ideal are they? Either way… no matter. Soon or later all these memories.. all these moments will be lost in time… vanished forever… like turds… in… a… drain."

"I knew you were going to say that. Anyway, according to my research you were a hardcore Serialist and disciple of the hypotheses of J.W. Dunne so that doesn't make any sense?"

"Oh yeah… forget that. I'll think of something else. Hang on." He went fumbling in his pockets with his shitty fingers "Time for a brew I reckon. Where's my other fucking tea-bag? I had two," he went. As last words went it was an improvement over all that wanky bullshit just before.

So I shot the cunt like I said I would. Death was instantaneous, his life switched off instantly, as bodily functions ceased on disconnection from a life support machine when there is no hope left. It was real ugly. Reader, I would feign spare you the details but my pen must have its voice. His noggin exploded in a dense cloud of grey and pink that exploded like an atomic bomb inna unmixed metaphor stylee. Bits of neural tissue spattered on dusty tomes, tiny little bone fragments razor sharp embedding in the soft half-calf. The cerebrum pretty much disintegrated but chunks of central stem were more resilient and the optic chiasm blasted skyward to the lamp fitting, sizzzling as it hit the lamp. The last I saw of the medulla oblongata it was whizzing down the aisle like a fucking rocket, or one of the little guys from out of *Fiend without a Face*. Sweeeet!

04:10:1963

On 20 January 2009, Barack Hussein Obama II assumed office as the 44th President of the USA. Obviously, the first thing he did when he got chance was to invite Beatle Paul to the White House which he did on 2nd June 2010 to award him the Gershwin Prize for Popular Song. Paul played a banging set for the President, supported by Corinne Bailey Rae and Herbie Hancock on "Blackbird" but disappointingly he didn't do "Piggies", presumably because that was one of George's.

Of course, if you were on the receiving end of a drone strike on the other side of the world then the colour of the president's skin didn't matter any more than the colour of his eyes... but yours almost certainly did. Which recalls the words of His Imperial Majesty, Lord of Lords, King of Kings, conquering Lion of the Tribe of Judah. Jah Rastafari I. Light of the World. Elect of Himself. Believed the personification of Divinity by His Children, Haile Selassie I spoke to the United Nations General Assembly on 4 October 1963, fewer than fifty days before JFK was killed. His speech was quoted by Bob Marley for his immortal tune *War*. Originally given in Ethiopia's official Amharic language at the UN, an English translation had been included in *Important Utterances of H.I.M. Emperor Haile Selassie I 1963-1972* and The Book gave permission to freely use its contents: "Any portion of this book could be reproduced by any process without permission."*

Bob most famously performed the rousing tune at independence celebrations in Zimbabwe in 1980 in a haze of tear gas, and in 2000 French producer Bruno Blum put out a CD of remixes of His Majesty's speech in various translations and arrangements, some featuring Bob Marley and The Wailers.

Many Rastas can recite His Majesty's speech from memory. It's the closest thing to a manifesto for Roots Reggae, the most influential musical form of the twentieth century.

* It's tempting to think that His Imperial Majesty forewent royalties out of generosity but perhaps he mindful of what happened in the city of Maqdala in 1868 when Britain sent a punitive expedition of 13,000 soldiers led by Sir Robert Napier and they ransacked the city killing 700 people and injuring thousands. The city was razed and Emperor Tewodros II committed suicide rather than be captured. The ancient churches and libraries were looted of their countless treasures and holy books and the booty was carried off on fifteen elephants and two hundred donkeys. It was so obscene a crime that Prime Minister Gladstone complained in Parliament about it to the army but to no avail. The swag was distributed to various pals and museums and libraries and virtually all of it still remains there, off limits to the public. Given the impossibility of resuscitating the dead it seems that our remaining obligations are quite clear. Intellectual property is one thing but this is another thing altogether. If His Imperial Majesty had been able to access to those holy manuscripts it would undoubtedly have helped defend Ethiopia against Mussolini's fascists in 1935.

I hesitated to include this footnote here because I did not want the overall tone of this book to trivialise this very serious issue. However, since this matter is currently so little known, I felt compelled to bring it your attention with due respect to all parties concerned.

I told you about that. The Rastafari livity originated with Leonard Howell in the Pinnacle Settlement in Kingston Jamaica in 1939. The lowest of the low. Outcast charcoal gatherers and broom-makers. In 1960, invited by Prince Buster, Count Ossie and his Nyabinghi brethren from Wareika Hills cut "Oh Carolina" the most influential record of the twentieth century and the world would never be the same again. It never had been.

QUIT WHILE YOU'RE AHEAD

"QUIET PLEASE!" Came an annoyed bellow from the Authoritarian Librarian who must have been hiding out the back now. Then I realised the silencer must have failed and the shot had rung out like a bang or a gunshot. I looked down at the piece in my hand and noticed I had pissed myself. What the fuck was it with all the pissing and shitting going on? The piss seemed to be a bit bloodshot and then I noticed a cock and balls lying on the ground by the recapitated old writer. I thought it should read decapitated.

"Fucking hell!" I was truly astonished. "He was so hardcore on the porn thing that he kept a spare cock and balls inside his cranial cavity. Not even The Bastardizer does that! As far as I know. I don't do that! Who does that?"

The old bastard sat up suddenly and staggered to his feet.

"Nug ggrrrr faarrrpp!! GGGAAAHHH!" He went, obviously confused.

"What exactly the fuck is happening?" I inquired. I was obviously hallucinating a lot of this. I just couldn't work out how much. Some cunt must have spiked me.

"Fuck me! The time machine worked!!" Explained The New Novelist. It turned out that it was the old writer only from another timeline where he had actually perfected his experiments. Which one? Who knows? Pick a number. The Bastardizer was impressed and a bit disconcerted to say the least.

"You should have seen that coming mate!" Added the novelist. "Hugh Everett's many-worlds interpretation (M WI) proves that there must be at least one future where his ideas would work and I would come back and do this. It was inevitable."

The Bastardizer levelled his piece with a shaking hand against the ostensible phantom. But then he lowered it again.

"What? Wasn't his lad in The Eels? They had some nice tunes…"

"Although Everett's ideas are patent nonsense in this continuum, I am from one where they proved… viable."

"What the fuck are you talking about you maniac!? What ideas? What continuum? Not viable? You should

I KNOW EXACTLY WHAT I'M DOING!!!

know… you invented the fucking Chron-O-Funnel™, you bastard!!!!"

The writer cackled maniacally for a moment and then said "Oh yeah.. I forgot you didn't know."

"Didn't know what?"

"You shot the wrong bloke… That guy was just a bum. He never invented nothing. Pissed his life away. He wrote dirty books and it sent him insane. You're in the wrong continuum. I fucking invented the Chron-O-Funnel™ you fuckwit!"

"That's what I fucking said you fucking shitheel!" I went and raised my piece again but as I steadied his aim momentarily—as I delusively believed I'd been trained to do—the New Novelist cunt reached behind him lightning quick and pulled a terrifying black turd as hard as a rock and flung it at The Bastardizer unexpectedly. Again. It was more like a paperweight than a shit. It was terrifying to conceive that a human anus might have been capable of such faeces but I'm not shitting you… The New Novelist was shitting The Bastardizer! That was why he'd shot him in the first place! I just told you that. Anyway the heavy stool smacked the amateur assassin square between the eyes just as he pulled the trigger. His shot ricocheted off a nearby bookshelf with an extremely loud noise. Ironically, it was the 346.730 shelves. The deflected shot then proceeded to shatter the spinning ceiling fan which exploded into several deadly shards. Now that's fucking magic. It was a miracle nobody was killed.

Mind you The Bastardizer's cock and balls copped a nasty piece of shrapnel which shredded them nastily. It all happened in slow-motion if you were an insect.

"My cock and balls!" I whinged, wriggling, "I was going to use those!"

"Why?!" I wheezed out, "Whyyyyyyyyyyyyy??!"

"You have presumed to meddle with a world-change. Poor spider!" He explicated "Caught in the wheel of the inevitable! You have linked my name with futility. You are an incompetent murderer. I am sorry for you!" He rested one bony hand on his hip—it was entirely untheatrical. "And now I vent my terrible fury…"

"Terrible furry what?"

As last words went these were even worse than the deadbeat novelist's had been, but despite that The Bastardizer decided that without his cock and balls life wasn't worth living. Even though he hadn't used them in the entire book. So he died. The New Novelist didn't notice or give a shit either way and he continued babbling his gibberish: "Don't believe all that PR bullshit on my TV show. In truth, I'm an evil bastard. For if it pleased me, I would kill everyone everywhere" he went on, "including all of the read-ers of this book, and all the potential readers of this book. In short, every fucker who fucks with me. Ever. Behold! I make the world into the image of a smoking turd. Not even an actual smoking turd you gather, just an image of a smoking turd.

"But I choose to grow weary now. Weary of all you cunts. And thus I exit this tome as suddenly as I came and continue my mission to impregnate every lifeform in this universe with my incredible seed! And also any ones on the International Space Station and that moonbase that will never be built now. And not only that but also I will kill every mortal upon their age of majority. It'll be like *Logan's Run*. And I'll take my shirt off! PHWOOAARRGH!"

It was probably just as well that the cops arrived at that point.

FALSE ENDING

Sadly, albeit predictably, things failed to improve for the old masturbologist despite the ludicrous lengths he had gone to. He was fitted up for The Bastardizer's murder in a Guantánamo Bay-themed Kangaroo Court and was lucky to end up in a loony bin instead of a gulag.

Like many prisoners of conscience, the old bastard refused to wear the prison uniform so they stripped him naked and denied him toilet facilities like they always do. He ended up having to smear his shit all over the walls so the guards wouldn't push his face into it. As I mentioned, his turds were very robust so he could use them like magic markers. In these unhygienic conditions he didn't last long and when he croaked from dysentery they came to hose the walls down and were amazed to see that what was written there was genius.

They photographed it meticulously to preserve the masturdpieces. The greatest conservationists in the immediate vicinity worked to develop a special varnish to preserve the precious frescoes for Eternity. He became a cloacal hero and his dank and lonely cell was soon a foecal attraction for copro-pilgrims. The income from it meant that the other prisoners didn't have to assemble Christmas crackers any more. Other prisons installed copies of the frescoes, sometimes improvising on the themes. Other experimental novelists that had found themselves imprisoned adopted his techniques. In the world outside, so-called free people started ripping off the idea like that craze for wearing your trousers hanging around your arse if you remember that. That was odd wasn't it? Anyway. Eventually shit-covered rooms became de rigueur and all over the world the ultra-fashionable pursued their new and unhygienic hobby. Inevitably coprophilia became the dominant cultural paradigm and so it was that human shit rendered all books, films, music and everything else obsolete.

12 December 2002
– 14 August 2013

THIS PAGE INTENTIONALLY LEFT BLANK

They ritually combusted the poor old fuck with a rare copy of *Razzle*, a half-kilo sack of tortilla chips and a six-pack of Budvar. He wasn't complaining. One mourner generously threw in a couple of hefty spliffs but no-one remembered to throw in a lighter because they were all thoughtless bastards. Then they took his mortal remains and lobbed them on the beach beneath that statue he liked so he could finally get some decent kip. Some crusties nearby had a bonfire going and were banging out old punk and roots standards on a ghettoblaster. The tide was lapping up between the groynes. It was getting cold and dark so they all went home and lived happily ever after. Good night everybody. Everybody everywhere... Good night. x

THE
END

1 Goodman and Buchanan's "The Flying Saucer" was released in 1956. What else happened that year?

A John Lennon formed The Quarrymen with Eric Griffiths and Pete Shotton

B Elvis Presly's debut LP was released

c Fidel Castro landed in Cuba

D None of the above

2 Who took the cover photograph for *With The Beatles?*

A Robert Freeman

B Astrid Kirchherr

c Gered Mankowitz

D No-one knows

3 Which is the greatest *Dr Who* serial of all time?

A *The Green Death*

B *City of Death*

c *The Talons of Weng-Chiang*

D *The Devils*

4 Who did the cover for The Beatles' 1968 self-titled LP?

A Paul McCartney

B Richard Hamilton

c Klaus Voormann

D No-one did

5 Which of these chapter titles appear in "The Warren Commission Report" ?

A The Curtain Rod Story

B The Long and Bulky Package

c The Abortive Transfer

D None of the above

6 Which of these phrases appear in the classic implementation of the ELIZA program?

A "DON'T YOU BELIEVE THAT I CAN*"

B "WHAT DOES THAT DREAM SUGGEST TO YOU?"

C "DO YOU LIKE SCONES?"

D "I'M NOT SURE I UNDERSTAND YOU FULLY."

7 How many birds are mentioned in Edgar Broughton's "Evening Over Rooftops"

A None

B Three little ones

C Forty-nine

D It isn't clear

8 When the Leningrad Rock Club opened in 1981, who was member number one?

A Leonid Brezhnev

B Boris Grebenshikov

C Chuck Berry

D Kolya Vasin

9 Who hosted *Top of the Pops* on 12 March 1987

A Tony Blackburn

B Bill Drummond and Jimmy Cauty

C Mike Smith and Steve Wright

D Janice Long and John Peel

10 Which of these institutions acquired treasures from the looting of Maqdala?

A The British Library

B The Victoria and Albert Museum

C The National Army Museum

D All of the above and many more

YOU HAVE BEEN READING

Adreon, Franklin, dir. *Cyborg 2087* [film]. USA: United Pictures Corporation, 1966.

Ali, Tariq. *Marching in the Streets*. London: Bloomsbury, 1998.

Allingham, Philip V. *Dickens's 1842 Reading Tour: Launching the Copyright Question in Tempestuous Seas* https://victorianweb.org/authors/dickens/pva/pva75.html accessed 24/6/2007

Aphrodite's Child. *666*. [LP record] UK: Vertigo, 1972.

Baldwin, Craig, dir. *Sonic Outlaws* [film]. USA, 1995.

Ballard, J.G. "The Index." in *Bananas* #8, Summer 1977. London.

Baran, Madeleine. Copyright and Music: A History Told in MP3's by www.illegal-art.org accessed 3 July 2007

Barratt, Leonard. *The Rastafarians: Sounds of Cultural Dissonance*. Boston: Beacon Press, 1977.

Beastie Boys. *Paul's Boutique* [LP record]. USA: Beastie Boys Records/Capitol Records, 1989.

Beatles, The. *The Beatles* [The White Album] [LP record]. London: Apple records, 1968.

Beatles, The. *With The Beatles* [LP record]. London: London: Parlophone Records, 1963.

Beckerman, Ray, "Large Recording Companies vs. The Defenseless : Some Common Sense Solutions to the Challenges of the RIAA Litigations", The Judges Journal, American Bar Association, Summer 2008 Edition. Vol. 47 No. 3, Summer 2008

Bester, Alfred. *Golem[100]*. London: Pan Books, 1981.

Borowczyk, Walerian, dir. *Emmanuelle 5*. France: New Horizon Picture Corp, 1987.

Bradley, Lloyd. *Bass Culture :When Reggae Was King*. London: Penguin, 2001.

Bugliosi, Vincent, and Curt Gentry. *Helter Skelter*. Ringwood, Vic: Penguin Books, 1980.

Byrds, The. "He Was a Friend of Mine" [7 inch record] USA: Columbia Records, 1965.

Captain Scarlet, ep. 6, "Operation Time" [tv]. UK: Century 21 Television Productions, first broadcast 17 November 1967.

Carpenter, John. dir. *Dark Star* [film]. USA: Jack H. Harris Enterprises/USC, 1974.

Clay, Tom. "What the World Needs Now" [7 inch record]. Detroit: Motown Records, 1971.

[Costello, Shaun, dir.] *Her Total Response* [film]. USA, 1977.

Crabtree, Arthur. *Fiend Without a Face* [film]. UK: Producers Associates, 1957.

Damiano, Gerard, dir. *Deep Throat* [film]. USA, 1972.

Damiano, Gerard, dir. *Behind the Green Door* [film]. USA, 1972.

Danger Mouse. *The Grey Album* [compact disc]. USA, 2004.

Dean Gray. *American Edit* [Download album]. [USA?]: Homemade Records, 2005.

Dickens, Charles. *The Life and Adventures of Nicholas Nickleby*. London: Oxford University Press, 1950.

Doctor Who. "An Unearthly Child" [tv]. UK: BBC TV, first broadcast 24 November 1963.

Doctor Who. "Rose" [tv]. UK: BBC TV, first broadcast 26 March 2005.

Doctor Who. "The Chase, Episode 1" [tv]. UK: BBC TV, first broadcast 22 May 1965.

Dunne, J. W. *An Experiment with Time*. Third Revised Edition. London: Faber & Faber, 1939.

Dunne, J. W. *Nothing Dies*. London: Faber & Faber, 1940.

Dunne, J. W. *The Serial Universe*. London: Faber, 1934.

Dunne, J.W. *The New Immortality*. London: Faber & Faber, 1938.

Dylan, Bob. [Great White Wonder] [LP record]. USA, 1969.

Edgar Broughton Band, The. *The Edgar Broughton Band* [The Meat Album] [LP record]. UK: Harvest Records, 1971.

Farnsworth, Philo T., Hise, S., McLaren, C. "Liner notes to Stay Free's Illegal Art compilation CD." accessed 3 July 2007, <www.illegal-art.org>.

Filliou, Robert, Emmett Williams, Daniel Spoerri, Roland Topor. *An Annecdoted Topography of Chance*. London: Atlas Press, 1995.

Gardner, Martin. "The fantastic combinations of John Conway's new solitaire game 'life'". In *Scientific American* 223 (October 1970): 120-123.

Goldman, William Scott. "Berne-ing the Soviet Copyright Codes: Will the U.S.S.R. Alter Its Copyright Laws to Comply with the Berne Convention?" Penn State International Law Review: Vol. 8: No. 3, Article 4. (1990) Available at: http://elibrary.law.psu.edu/psilr/vol8/iss3/4

Goodman, Dickie and Bill Buchanan. "The Flying Saucer" [7 inch record] . USA: Luniverse, 1956.

Green Day. *American Idiot* [compact disc]. USA: Reprise Records, 2004.

Haile Selassie. featuring Bob Marley. *The War Album* [compact disc]. France: Rastafari Records, 2000.

Haile Selassie. *Important Utterances of H.I.M.* Addis Ababa: Imperial Ethiopian Ministry Of Information, 1972.

Harrison, George. *All Things Must Pass* [LP record]. UK: Apple Records, 1970.

Heylin, Clinton. *Bootleg! The Rise and Fall of the Secret Recording Industry*. London: Omnibus Press, 2003.

Hill, Mildred. *Song Stories for the Kindergarten*. Chicago: Clayton F. Summy, 1896.

HM Government. *Copyright Act, 1956*. London: HMSO, 1956.

Home, Stewart, ed. *Mind Invaders : A Reader in Psychic Warfare, Cultural Sabotage and Semiotic Terrorism*. London: Serpent's Tail, 1997.

Home, Stewart. *Plagiarism: Art as Commodity and Strategies for its Negation*. n.p.: Aporia Press, 1987.

Jay-Z. *The Black Album (Acapella) (Explicit)*. [LP record]. USA: Roc-A-Fella Records, 2003.

Rouner, Jef. *The History of The Beatles In Doctor Who*, Houston Press, accessed 20 July 2013, < https://www. houstonpress.com/music/the-history-of-the-beatles-in-doctor-who-6514814>

Jones, Chuck, dir. *Hare-Way to the Stars* [short film]. USA: Warner Bros., 1958.

Justified Ancients of Mu Mu. [All You Need is Love] [White label 12"]. [UK: KLF Communications, 1987.]

Justified Ancients of Mu Mu. *1987 What the Fuck Is Going On?* [LP record]. Aylesbury: KLF Communications, 1987.

Katz, David. *People Funny Boy: The Genius of Lee Scratch Perry*. Edinburgh: Payback Press, 2000.

King Koba [Lee Perry]. "Station Underground News" [7 inch record]. Jamaica: Undergound, 1973.

Kubrick, Stanley, dir. *2001: A Space Odyssey* [film]. UK: MGM, 1968.

Kubrick, Stanley, dir. *Dr. Strangelove or: How I Learned to Stop Worrying and Love the Bomb* [film]. UK: Columbia Pictures, 1964.

Landis, John, dir. *The Blue Brothers* [film]. USA: Universal Pictures, 1980.

Lockwood, Louise. dir. *Parallel Worlds, Parallel Lives*. [tv] UK: BBC TV, first broadcast: 26 November 2007.

Lord Rock and Time Boy. [Cauty, James and Bill Drummond.] *The Manual (How to Have a Number One the Easy Way)*. Wendover, Buckinghamshire: KLF Publications, 1988.

Magazine. *Rays & Hail 1978 - 1981* [CD album] . UK: Virgin Records, 1987.

Man 2 Man Meets Man Parrish. "Male Stripper (New U.K. Mix)" [12 inch record]. UK: Bolts Records, 1986.

Markie, Bix. *I Need a Haircut* [LP record]. USA: Warner Bros. Records, 1991.

Moles Abraham, Antoine, and Ephraim Cohen Joel. *Information Theory and Aethetic Perception*. London: Illinois University Press, 1966.

Negativland. *Escape from Noise* [LP record]. SST Records, Lawndale, 1987.

Negativland. *Fair Use: The Story of the Letter U and the Numeral 2*. Concord, CA: Seeland, 2000.

Negativland. *Guns* [12 inch record]. Lawndale, CA: SST, 1996.

Negativland. *Helter Stupid* [LP record]. Lawndale, CA: SST, 1989.

Negativland. *U2* [12 inch record]. SST Records, Lawndale, 1991.

O'Brien, Damien and Brian Fitzgerald "Mashups, remixes and copyright law." *Internet Law Bulletin* 9(2):pp. 17-19. (2006).

Ormond, Ron, dir. *If Footmen Tire You What Will Horses Do?* [film] USA: The Ormond Organization, 1971.

Otfonoski, Steve, *The Golden Age of Novelty Songs*. New York: Billboard Books, 2000.

Pankhurst, Richard. *Maqdala and Her Loot*. AFROMET - The Association for the Return of The Maqdala

Ethiopian Treasures, accessed 6 December 2008, <http://www.afromet.org:80/history/>

Perry, Marsha. *Struggles for Copyright Law,* Charles Dickens Gad's Hill Place, accessed 24 June 2007, <http://www.perryweb.com/Dickens/work_copy.shtml >.

President's Commission on the Assassination of President Kennedy. *The Warren Commission Report*. New York: St Martin's Press, 1992.

Priestley, J. B. *Man and Time*. London: Aldus Books, 1964.

Priestley, J.B. *An Inspector Calls. A Play in Three Acts.* London, Toronto: William Heinemann, 1947.

Prince. The Black Album [LP record]. USA: Warner Bros. Records, 1987.

Public Enemy. *It Takes a Nation of Millions to Hold Us Back* [LP record]. USA: Def Jam Recordings, 1988.

Public Enemy. *Revolverlution* [LP record]. USA: Slam Jamz/Koch Records, 2002.

Razzle. Vol. 4. No. 23. London: Paul Raymond Publications, 1986.

Rimmer, M. (2005), "The Grey Album: Copyright Law and Digital Sampling", pp. 40-53 in *Media International Australia* 114 (Feb) (Special issue on Copyright, Media and Innovation).

Saint-Exupéry, Antoine. *The Little Prince*. London: Piccolo, 1982.

Schneiderman, Davis. "Everybody's Got Something to Hide Except for Me and My Lawsuit: William S. Burroughs, DJ Danger Mouse, and the Politics of 'Grey Tuesday'". In *Plagiary* I (2006): 191-206

Shaposhnikov, Igor. *Brothers in Mind. Early Phase* [in Russian], accessed 10 September 2020, <https://specialradio.ru/art/id311/ >.

Southgate, Vera, Robert Lumley, Jacob Grimm, and Wilhelm Grimm. *The Elves and the Shoemaker*. Loughborough, England: Ladybird Books, 1965.

Stallman, Richard, and Joshua Gay. *Free Software, Free Society : Selected Essays of Richard M. Stallman*. Boston, Mass.: GNU Press, 2002.

Stanton, Andy, and David Tazzyman. *You're a Bad Man, Mr. Gum!* London: Egmont, 2006

Steinski & The Mass Media. *The Motorcade Sped On* [12 inch record]. USA: Tommy Boy Records, 1986.

Sterne, Laurence, and Ian C. Ross. *The Life and Opinions of Tristram Shandy, Gentleman*. Oxford : Oxford University Press, 1983.

Strong, Simon. *A259 Multiplex Bomb "Outrage"*. Hove: CodeX, 1995.

Stump. *A Fierce Pancake* [LP record]. UK: Ensign Records, 1988.

Tehranian, John. "Infringement Nation: Copyright Reform and the Law/Norm Gap." In *Utah Law Review*. No. 3 p537-549

Timelords, The. *Doctorin' the Tardis* [12 inch record]. UK: KLF Communications, 1988.

Top of the Pops [Untitled tv episode]. UK: BBC TV, first broadcast 15 April 1965.

Top of the Pops [Untitled tv episode]. UK: BBC TV, first broadcast 12 March 1987.

Troitsky, Artemy. *Tusovka: Who's Who In The New Soviet Rock Culture*. London: Omnibus, 1990.

Vaidhyanathan, Siva. *After the copyright smackdown: What next?* Salon.com , accessed 22 January 2003, <http://www.salon.com/tech/feature/2003/01/17/copyright/print.html>.

Various artists. *Illegal Art Exhibit Companion CD* [compact disc]. USA: Stay Free!/Illegal Art, 2002.

Various artists. *Nuggets II: Original Artyfacts From The British Empire And Beyond 1964-1969*. [compact disc box set]. USA: Rhino Records, 2001.

Watson, Charles, and Ray Hoekstra. *Will You Die For Me?*
    Old Tappan, N.J.: F.H. Revell, 1978.

Weizenbaum, Joseph. *Computer Power and Human Reason:
    From Judgement to Calculation*. Harmondsworth: Pen-
    guin Books, 1976.

Weizenbaum, Joseph. "ELIZA – A Computer Program
    For the Study of Natural Language Communication
    Between Man and Machine." Cambridge, Mass: *Com-
    munications of the ACM* Vol. 9, No. 1 (January 1966):
    36-35.

White Album Project, The. *A comprehensive look at The
    Beatles self-titled double-album masterpiece*, accessed 19
    July 2013, <https://www.thewhitealbumproject.
    com/ >.

Wishman, Doris, dir. *Satan Was a Lady* [film]. USA, 1975.

Zapruder, Abraham. [Zapruder Film of Kennedy Assassi-
    nation.] [Super 8 film]. Prod. Dallas, 1963.

CONTENTS

CRIPPLEGATE BOOKS

Certificate
OF COMPLETION

This is to certify that

has read and enjoyed a copy of
THE BASTARDIZER POLISHES A TURD
by "Chus Martinez"

signed   "CHUS MARTINEZ"

dated

DENIZEN OF THE DEAD

THE HORRORS OF CLARENDON COURT
EDITED BY STEWART HOME

— WARNING! —

You are about to enter the City of London,
the most evil and corrupt place on the planet!

On the border between the City's Cripplegate ward and south Islington's Bone Hill district stands Clarendon Court AKA The Denizen - an elite and newly built luxury apartment block of 99 flats marketed to property investors.

Exclusive? Yes.
Reassuringly expensive? Yes.
Safe? Undoubtedly not!

There were stories, just rumours, about what went on there. Rumours about perversion, orgies, ghosts, bad feng shui and shockingly unpleasant deaths.

When a gorgeous young nymphomaniac bursts into a Clarendon Court apartment, the whole story of depravity and corruption is revealed.

In this collection of short fiction by today's top writers the Clarendon Court investment flats really are haunted by the ghosts of Cripplegate's wild past, when the hood was notorious for its brothels and the ultra-violent criminals who frequented them.

On top of this there's a problem with the spirits of hundreds of thousands of unhappy souls whose corpses were dumped in both local plague pits and the more recent Golden Lane mega-morgue, a huge Victorian Palace of the Dead.

This anthology is a protest against property speculation and a new take on the genre of haunted house horror fiction. The book itself is a talisman that defends our communities against developers and inside it also features Spell Series by the w.o.n.d.e.r. coven. The symbols of this living spell are a lock and key designed to dismantle the neoliberal project and overdevelopment as represented by The Denizen.

Featuring work from
Paul Ewen, Tariq Goddard,
Iphgenia Baal, Chris Petit,
Steve Finbow, John King,
Chloe Aridjis, Tom McCarthy,
Liz Rever, Katrina Palmer,
Michael Hampton,
Bridget Penney,
Stewart Home
and many more!

BARON'S COURT, ALL CHANGE

TERRY TAYLOR

INTRODUCED BY STEWART HOME

Baron's Court, All Change is the Holy Grail of beatnik novels, Terry Taylor's book documents one summer in the life of an unnamed sixteen year-old narrator. Leaving home and his job he dabbles in spiritualism, is seduced by an older woman and gets rich quick from drug dealing. This is a world of sharp suits, jazz, kicks, "spades", nightclubs and sex. A London that is already swinging half a decade before the rest of the world catches on.

Terry Taylor (1933-2014) was the much younger lover of Ida Kar, whose National Portrait Gallery collection includes a series of photographs of Terry getting stoned in London's Soho back in 1956. His proto-mod exploits as a young man are fictionalised in Colin MacInnes' famous novel *Absolute Beginners*. Throughout Taylor's life music, magic rituals and hallucinogenic drugs loomed large. Terry spent time in Goa and hung out with William Burroughs in Tangier before settling down in the wilds of north Wales, where he continued to dig modern jazz and perfect his occult practices.

2021 (originally published 1961) / 5½×8½" / 208 pp

STEWART HOME

This is the story of Ray "The Cat" Jones who wanted to become middleweight boxing champion of the world but eventually made his mark as the greatest cat burglar of all time.

Ray is a modern-day Robin Hood waging a relentless class war against the rich. From the jewels of movie stars Elizabeth Taylor and Sophia Loren, to the private papers of the Duke of Windsor, paintings by Rubens and Rembrandt, and the furs of the London aristocracy, Ray's carefully targeted burglaries are perfectly planned and thrillingly executed.

A vision of London's underworld from wartime to near present.

The narrative weaves between the clubs of Soho, populated by gangsters and gamblers, to the mansions of Kensington and Hampstead, inhabited by corrupt politicians and millionaires, and on into the dingy cells of the city's prisons.

2021 (originally published 2014) / 5½×8½" / 256 pp

STEWART HOME ✳ CRANKED UP REALLY HIGH

In this controversial new book, Stewart Home uses notions of genre lifted from film theory to prove that the Sex Pistols weren't a punk rock band. He follows this up by outlining a dialectic of punk rock that on a compressed time-scale mirrors the growth and decay of the major political ideologies of the past century. Home offers a devastating critique of those writers who have claimed that there is a link between punk and avant-garde art movements such as Situationism. He believes that it is the triviality of punk rock which makes it a viable opponent of serious culture.

Rather than reiterating the histories of well known groups, Home turns his attention to less well documented aspects of punk rock. As well as discussing sixties garage rock and the British, American and Finnish punk scenes of the late seventies, Home devotes whole chapters to deconstructing Riot Grrrl, Oi! and the sorry saga of Nazi bonehead band Skrewdriver.

Stewart Home is best known as the author of several critically acclaimed novels, the newest of which, entitled *Slow Death*, will be published by Serpent's Tail early next year. He is widely regarded as an authority on avant-garde art and, according to several sources, 'an egomaniac on a world historical scale'. Mr. Home is single and lives in London where he spends his time pursuing an interest in Hegelian philosophy and composing satirical magazine articles about the royal family.

A5 Paperback 128 pp.
1899588-01-4 £5.95

www.ingramcontent.com/pod-product-compliance
Lightning Source LLC
Chambersburg PA
CBHW070401200726
48294CB00003B/1024